I0575522

festive little fling

A Peacock Springs Spin-Off

Jordana Blake

just vibes media, llc*

Festive Little Fling

Copyright © 2025

just vibes media, llc*

Paperback ISBN: 979-8-9985325-3-5

Digital ISBN: 979-8-9985325-2-8

Editing & Proof Reading: Emilie Mortati, Glitter Penned Edits

Cover Design by Jillian Liota, Blue Moon Creative Studio

❀ Formatted with Vellum

dear reader,

The following story is a spin-off from the Peacock Springs series, a product of my undying love for TV/movies of the late 1990s and early 2000s and psychology. Within these pages *Festive Little Fling* takes all of the fun parts of a 'typical' JB story and leaves the traum-com for another day. If you'd like to meet Shae's sister and brother-in-law, Fighting can be found on Amazon or at Scribbles Bookshop.

Growing up I used to have the most intense Christmas envy. I hated that my family wasn't included in the magic around me and I found company in a middle grade book, The Christmas Revolution' by Barbara Cohen. The arrival of a new boy, Simeon, to this school changes how one Jewish girl sees the season. Simon was (possibly) my first *book boyfriend*, so this hottie who can cook is in honor of him.

While there aren't any major triggers to note, please be advised the following sensitive subjects are included: open door sex scenes, cannabis and alcohol use, and explicit language.

Please note there are multiple ways to experience real-life events and I have done my best, alongside my team, to do it justice. Though you may not relate—it does not make it untrue.

While I hope you love my imaginary friends, your mental health should always come first. Please be kind to your mind.

Happy Reading,

Jordana

for everyone who has been envious of Christmas,
why don't we make our own magic this year?

shae

SLIDING into the business class seat, I swipe a sanitizing wipe over the arms, tray, and all knobs. It was in my hand before I sat down.

"Have an extra? Those smell lovely," a white-bearded, round elderly gentleman, who is way-too-jolly for this early, asks me.

Holding out the green package, he glances down and takes a deep inhale. "Pine, of course I like it. My favorite scent." He gives a playful wink before taking one from the package and similarly cleaning his tray table and armrests.

The flight crew walks the narrow aisle holding out a clear trash bag, collecting wipes and other random bits of trash from passengers before preparing for takeoff. The chipper septuagenarian holds his palm out toward me and says, "Saul, Saul Nichlause. Let me." He motions for me to hand my wipe to him, and I accept the kind gesture.

"Thanks, I'm Shae. Like where the Mets used to play," I say while I try to connect my blue tooth headphones to my phone. I hope the international signal for please don't talk to me will translate to getting a little sleep on this flight. So far, I have no luck.

1

"Flying from Philadelphia but bringing up the old Mets stadium? You must be a very brave girl," he says and winks conspiratorially.

"Can't change my namesake just because we're in enemy territory, now, can I?" I say with a bit of a sly smile in return. Well, if this isn't going to be a nap, it better be a damn good story.

"What's got you on the outbound route? I would assume the snowbirds went back to Miami in October..." I trail off, realizing there's a chance I offend him with the end of this statement. I would expect someone retired to be inbound to Philadelphia for Christmas with family, not outbound.

"They did indeed, and I am not sure I count as a snowbird these days. I'm a full time Floridian; I had some business to take care of in New York earlier in the week. I stopped by some old friends for a night, and I'm headed home. What about you, slugger?" he asks, transitioning the conversation so smoothly I find myself locked in despite my previous desire to sleep.

"I work for a public relations firm in Philly, and one of our larger clients is organizing a major New Years Eve event. When the team in Miami found out that someone's adorable toddler exposed the entire team there to Coxsackievirus—that's the hand, foot, and mouth..." I trail off and a shudder of fear rolls through me. Saul is a mirror to my disgusted expression.

"So, as a token member of the tribe and someone desperately vying for a promotion in the new year, I volunteered to be the person on the ground. It's honestly a pretty sweet deal. I have a handful of check ins, but I also get to avoid the big-family drama over Christmas and work on my tan," I say. "I might even use this time to check out the rest of the Miami scene, there's supposed to be a lot of great parties all week."

"You're at Shine?" Mr. Nichlause asks, referring to Emily Shine, one of the leading public relations professionals in the world. Her rolodex of clients—and yes Emily still uses a pen and

2

paper so nobody can hack in and get her clients private contact information—includes some of the most well-known actors and musicians around. She is also extremely private about her whereabouts at any given time, and the viral outbreak in our southern office leaking would be bad news for me.

"I didn't say that," I reply, shrugging one shoulder.

Mr. Nichlause taps on my tablet, and the screen shows the layout I've been reviewing for my first stop. There's also a giant red *confidential* notice and our company logo.

Pushing one wrinkled pointer finger to his lips, he makes the international sign for quiet. "Don't worry, your secret is safe with me. I was in the biz' myself back in the day," he says, his kind eyes suggesting he's telling the truth.

"Well, at least that was before I met the members of Fleetwood Mac."

Hearing Stevie Nicks and I shook the same hand has me perking up in my seat. I think he can tell he's hooked me through the change in my body language.

"You met Fleetwood?" I gasp.

He chuckles and shakes his head. "Not just Mick. Lindsay, John, Stevie, and Christine too. Those were some wild days let me tell you. There is always a crisis to kill when you work in public relations alongside anyone in the music industry. But that crew; that was a master class. Imagine what folks didn't hear."

We share a laugh and then he grows more somber. "I like you, kid. Listen, I've got a special place in my heart for any fellow chaos wrangler. Take my card so that if you need anything while in town you can call me. I know just about everyone you could need in an emergency."

My heart is speeding up. This Santa-looking man could be exactly what I need to ensure I wow everyone this week. The plane begins to taxi the runway, and he pulls out an oversized pair of red headphones. I do the same, putting my earbuds in and taking a deep breath. Take off is my least favorite part of flying, so I begin to recite to myself the list of things I want to get out of this trip.

One. Recognition for stepping up.

Two. A tan.

Three. Get laid to kill some of this stress.

simon

"ARE you out of your minds, gentlemen?" I yell first in English, then Spanish, to ensure the entire kitchen staff knows I'm *not* playing.

"Chef, I'm sorry but Uncle Eli is here and so are the delivery trucks. Can we put a pin in this?" my right hand and younger sister Bekah says.

"Shit, already?" I yell. I look down at my watch unable to comprehend that it's this late.

"You go deal with deliveries and I'll stall Uncle E. Okay?" She shoos me out the kitchen toward our delivery doors with a flick of the wrist.

As I approach, there is the distinct, loud metallic bang of the door knocking into the stair railing.

"Simon, hey there. Ready for the holiday rush?" the driver asks. He's our usual guy, so we've got a friendly thing going. Or we did. Looking at the produce crates he dropped onto my table has me panicking.

"What is this?" I bite, sharper than he deserves knowing he didn't pack the truck.

"What's the problem this week?" he says with a sigh, his good nature unflappable as usual.

"Well, these are definitely not pomegranates," I grumble.

Flipping through his sheet he locates a spot on both paper and crate. "Looks like someone ordered Chinese Apples, which this is clearly marked as."

"Fucking hell," I rumble because this is the sort of stupid mistake that only one man would make. As I'm trying to figure out how to handle this massive inconvenience to my menu, I hear the heavy footsteps and no-nonsense push back against Bekah.

"Rebekah, dear, I appreciate what you're saying but I am the *owner* of this establishment," his husky smokers voice retorts.

"*Silent* partner," she says in a muffled tone, but I catch it from a distance.

Waving a hand at her, Eli enters the room with wide arms. "There's my boy genius! Come here, Simon!" He approaches me for a hug. It's as affable and boisterous as his entrance.

Grabbing a piece of fruit from the crate, Eli shines it on his shirt. "I have impeccable timing kid. Thanks," he says before he takes a bite.

"Can you swing by with the pomegranates too? I'll sign. Clipboard?" I say with a grumble before signing off on the delivery. My thoughts start to sift through what menu items may need to be replaced.

"So, listen, you know the catering company is handling that celebrity event on New Years. I know you're too big for that now, what with your James Beard award and the Michelin Stars, but I might need you. So, keep the night open, okay?" He places his bear paw sized hand on my shoulder and gives a good shake.

"Sure thing, Uncle Eli. I have to get back to prep for the week —my menu just changed. But hey! Enjoy the apple." I don't try to hide my sarcasm this time.

"Chin up, buttercup, there's going to be models and actresses at that shindig. Maybe you can find yourself someone to help you get over this shit mood. Or at least get you laid." He laughs at his own joke.

Watching my uncle stroll out the back door, a pack of cigarettes in hand and flicking his zippo lighter, makes me want a break too. His quip about getting laid is the last fucking straw, and I grumble to nobody. "This is fucking bullshit, I work non-stop, I'd love a chance to meet someone." I say before I reign in the thoughts to keep from sharing them.

I toss the bar towel over my shoulder and stare at my sister. "How are we even related to him again?"

"Need me to draw you the family tree?" she deadpans.

"No, I'd like to figure out what the *fuck* I'm going to do with all these *Asian Pears* that were ordered as "Chinese Apples" and are most definitely *not* pomegranates. Let me get into the office to tinker with some ideas. Can you keep them fixing the issues with the walk in please? I'd hate to fire everyone before the big pre-holiday chef's table event."

"You wouldn't!" Bekah gasps.

Sighing, I glare. "Try me." The silly grin breaks before she's fully out of my line of sight.

shae

EXITING the black SUV ride share, I step down into the sunshine and immediately my muscles relax. The chill of a Philadelphia winter has melted away and immediately improved my mood.

Why do I still live up there? I should really consider a move to a warmer city. Jews are desert dwelling people, not built for cold.

Travel days can be the worst, but check in at the hotel went well enough that I'm hopeful it will be smooth sailing from here. Today is easy; I'll run down the list items before I go for a mani-pedi. I get to spend Christmas doing whatever I want this year. Which means I'm going between the pool and a king-size bed with room service. Plus, my kindle is full and my favorite vibrator is charging in the event I don't find someone else to spend the evening with.

It can't get better than this, can it? I swipe a text notification away without reading it because: yes. It can get better. I also get to miss the insanity that is Nessa and Mateo's Chrismukkah party. As much as I'm glad to be in a better place than years past, sometimes it's better to get to step out of *little miss perfect's* shadow.

It's one of many reasons the rest of the family is across the river from me. I'm tired of the scrutiny. It's exhausting. I'm different from everyone in our family. I'm done feeling bad about it. Letting out an irritated scoff I push all the family drama to the side.

Our venue is a modern art deco estate, with palm trees lining the walkway. It's well paved and smooth, which is good for clientele who will likely be in designer heels. The white stucco mixed with glass and soft wood accents present glamour day or night, but I cannot wait to see this place lit up under the navy skies.

Reaching into my leather bag, I pull out my tablet and digital pen. Bringing up the team checklist, I give it a cursory scan. First thing I notice in the entryway are wrapped pallets from the previous event. They were due to be picked up early this morning, and checking the time on the clock, 9:19 AM, it no longer counts as early. Pausing in my tracks, I dial the transportation company and tap my toes to the hold music.

"Hi, thank you for waiting. How can I help you?" someone finally says.

"Yes, hi. I'm standing at the entryway to Devotional and the items your team were supposed to remove are still here. I wanted to confirm if the drivers are en route?" I ask in my professional phone voice.

I hear the clicking of nails on a keyboard and send out a silent prayer for good news.

"I'm sorry, The Devotional? It looks like our team was already there. Are you sure this was for us?" she asks sounding confused. I read off the information on the transit slip and she clicks around on the keys some more. "No, I'm sorry miss but we do not have anything that matches that information. That may have been left from the pickup?"

I have no other clue as to what this might be, it's so tightly wrapped in cellophane all I can confirm is there is a pallet. "Never mind, I'll figure it out." My voice is more clipped than I would have liked, but now I'm digging around for something sharp enough to pierce the wrapping.

Before I can get the point of my pen through the outer layer I hear someone shouting at me from far away. The emptiness of the space means that everything echoes and reverberates off the walls. I see a group of short, tan men jogging toward me with the one at the front waving his hands and shouting.

"Miss, no. Please don't." I raise my hands and step back showing that I heard them.

"Slow down, I'm not in a rush," I call.

"Hi, I'm Enrique, I'm from the venue team." He extends a large, calloused hand to me. I can see traces of black ink at the neck of his T-shirt, and his masculine scent from the hard work is powerful. His forearms flex as we shake hands, showing off the sinuous muscles. I will be adding this image to the spank bank for later, thank you Enrique. I'm so lost in the lust filled fantasy I zone out for a moment.

"And you are?" he says while dropping my hand that held his a bit too long.

"Oh, hi. I'm Shae, from Shine PR. I'm here to lead the first wave of set up." I shake off my thoughts and jump into work mode.

"Shine PR? Didn't expect them to send someone so young down. Well, let me give my crew their marching orders and I'll show you around." He turns and calls out instructions to the team.

"Right this way." He extends an arm toward the opposite hallway from the retreating crew. As the team continues to unload the truck filled with seating, we enter into the wing where the luxury spa and change rooms are. We weave through the open space onto a deck lined with plunge pools. Winding our way to the reflecting pool the path divides leading to a tropical garden, a staff center, and a series of onsite bungalows for overnight guests.

Using the middle path, we continue on to the staff building where a pretty boring office greets us. There's a closet that has an industrial sized washer and dryer next to linen storage, a copy machine that won't stop beeping, and a few desktop computers scattered around.

"This is the area the Shine Team will have reserved for the rest of the week after the holidays. If you need to set up for Emily there is also a nice conference room that can be converted to a private office behind you." I turn and see the circular table and TV. It'll do.

"Thanks, Enrique," I say while unpacking some of my things onto the desk before me. "Are there any access codes or passes I'll need?" Taking a pad from the desk, he writes down ten digits, then below them four more.

"That's my number if you need anything, and this is the building passcode." With a slight wave he returns to the crew.

"Wait! One more thing," I call, and he pauses at the door. "Did any wardrobe for the hosts get delivered?"

"The rolling rack is in the next conference room over." He points, winks, and saunters to the team unloading the truck.

Rushing into the tiny work room, I look over the rolling rack; it's filled from end to end with a variety of suits and gowns. I grab my tablet and pull up the email outlining the various outfits and the wardrobe changes the hosts planned for the evening. So far everything appears in order. That is until a tiny number on the tag catches my eye. The woman wearing these items could fit three times in the final piece—the star dress of the evening. Searching frantically, I look for the information on the designer, the fashion house rental, or anyone who might know something about this. Surely, they didn't mess up the most important item? It's not possible.

The phone rings and rings, but nobody answers. I glance at the clock; it's noon and my stomach is grumbling. I have an appointment for my nails later this afternoon, and I'll have to keep calling between the rest of the tasks. Arriving in the main area, I see a second crew has arrived as they move carts and crates toward the prep kitchen.

A series of horrible events happens all at once: the team unwraps the first of the couches, a group moving a series of large vases creates poor visibility, and one of the catering crew is rolling cases of red wine in on a dolly. The cement planter goes crashing into the wine, the wooden crates topple forward, and glass shatters everywhere. A river of Argentinian Malbec flows and I watch in horror as the chair absorbs stains.

A middle-aged man with a leather-like tan face starts to shout in a mix of languages at his crew as he stomps my way. My spine sharpens, shoulders square, ready to fight for him to immediately fix things. When he realizes I'm witnessing this entire debacle, he slows and softens his steps. The heavy furrow of his brow relaxes and a smile spreads that does not quite reach his eyes. With gray curly hair a bit unruly and a pack of old school smokes showing in his button down Hawaiian shirt pocket, he reminds me of Anthony Bourdain.

"Shae Rabin, with Shine PR," I say with as much power as I can muster while shoving my hand toward him for a shake.

"Our Shine rep? Wonderful," he shouts and clasps my hand, picking it up for a soft kiss on my knuckles. Like I'm royalty.

"And you are?" The question holds a slight bite, but I try to play nice.

"Sorry. Yes. I'm Eli Hakimi, head of catering for this event. It seems my crew was not paying enough attention and now you've got one foot in the Red Sea." He laughs at his own joke.

I look at my shoes, and sure enough there's red wine beginning to pool at the bottom of my most expensive nude heels. *Shit.*

I step to the side away from the spill and Eli follows. "I'll take care of all of this, don't worry. To make it up to you, why don't you take a reservation for tonight on me. I'll get you a seat at the chefs table at Sin, on the house. For all the trouble. Unless you need to go visit some grandparents for Christmas Eve? Headed to Boca?"

That finally breaks some of my building anxiety and a genuine laugh breaks free. "No, my plans were to spend these forty-eight hours lounging by the pool at the hotel until my boss arrives. You really can have this all fixed by the time she's here?" I ask, eyes darting around at the mess.

There's something so genuine, Eli reminds me of my uncles, so I want to trust him. I hope I'm making the right call.

"Absolutely, blondie. I've worked with The Devotional for years. I know the right people to get this done. You have a lot on that list there," he says while tapping toward my iPad.

"That is true," I waver.

"So, it's settled, you'll take the seat at Sin tonight. Tell Simon I sent you. Go. Go. You have other things to get to." He is insistent and somehow, I find myself convinced. I open my phone to add the time and location into my calendar before running to the cab to my next stop while calling about that dress.

simon

"WHAT DO you mean you need me to add a seat tonight?" I shout at my Uncle Eli over the noise of the kitchen prep.

It's one of the busiest nights since we've opened Sin and this is just like him.

"Listen, there was a little incident today when my guys were bringing the wine to Devotional, so I needed to give an apology to the PR coordinator there. She looked like she was about to take my nuts off," he says, then gives me a single shoulder shrug, as if to tag on a silent *what can you do?*

"So you invited this ballbuster into my dining room for a personalized experience with me? That seems like a great idea," I say with a grimace.

"Who covered your initial investment, Simon?" Uncle Eli asks, knowing this will end the conversation.

"So that was a seat for one. What time?" I ask hoping to ignore the conversation about start-up funds.

"Last seating. And Si, she's cute. Young. In town alone too. Could be fun for you too, workaholic," he says poking again at the topic of my sex life.

Slamming a burnt caramel pan into the sink with a sizzle, I

14

turn and shout, "You got your way, now get out of mine. Go. I have work to do. And where the fuck is the prep team?"

"Here boss," my sous chef shouts as they tie on an apron.

"About damn time. Looks like we'll need to increase the prep for the tasting menu to include an extra person now," I say as I glare at my uncle's retreating form.

THE KITCHEN IS hotter than usual tonight. Correction: The kitchen is hotter than a volcano erupting inside hell tonight.

We've seated all the planned tables and now I'm waiting for Uncle Eli's guest to arrive. I can't explain why but I'm positive this is part of my excessive sweating tonight. A cute woman traveling solo over the holidays with no plans. It doesn't add up.

When the doors open a few minutes later, the air outside wafts in and sends a jolt through me. I'm placing a small bite intermezzo before the older couple I've been entertaining in hopes of getting investors to expand and nearly drop the spoons filled with sorbetto on the wife's lap.

A tiny woman with curvy hips and a long blonde ponytail cascading down her back stands in the doorway. Her dark green dress is short, really short, and so tight. Her skin has the pinkish glow of a fresh tan. While everyone else around here is bundled up for our chilly December temperatures in the high fifties, she's holding an oversized lightweight blazer over one arm. Fuck she's hot. Please be my special guest.

I hear my hostess greeting her but the dinner conversation obstructs my ability to eavesdrop on the response.

"Chef, this is our final seating for your table tonight," the hostess says as she waves the beauty over.

"Hi," she says holding out a hand and giving a firm shake. While our hands are clasped, her honey brown eyes find mine. In my head, I'm a cartoon character and my eyes have popped out of my head and exploded. My cartoon mouth is open, tongue unrolling like the red carpet I should have laid at this angel's feet. My cartoon heart is beating so hard in my chest it leaves my body and flies in and out of me in a reckless pattern. Her thumb absentmindedly glides across the skin between my thumb and knuckles, and sparks heat through every pixel until Cartoon Simon has fully melted into a rain of squares. He's dead. I'm dead. The angel is talking to me.

"Thank you so much for squeezing me in, Chef, I know this was unexpected."

I try to swallow but my throat has gone dry. She drops my hand and heads directly to the high stool for the chef's table experience, winking over her shoulder.

Sliding into the seat, I watch her eyes glow in the flickering candlelight with flecks of amber and gold. Draped around her neck is a delicate chain, with a tiny hand-shaped pendant. It falls at the throat. It gives me an eyeful of her expansive neck and the petite bump of cleavage. Wow, that is some view. Swallowing thickly a second time, I stammer, "Beautiful necklace," then immediately turn and stomp off.

Beautiful necklace? Not *hi. Not I'm Simon, yes you know that. Not thanks for coming. You cook for pretty girls all the time, Si, this is ridiculous. Get your shit together,* I chide internally as I head to the kitchen.

"Where are the mini Tahdig pots?" I shout as I check the prep area for them. The metal-on-metal clang as I lift and drop containers and lids matches the rattling of my pulse.

"Each one needs about an hour to properly set, and we're already on the final seating. They should be here trayed up," I say, dropping the final lid with a particularly strong bang.

"Already in their individual mini pots and over the burners on low with the lids wrapped in a towel, chef," a prep cook calls to me.

There's a small sizzle as pans are moved around the stove top at high heat, and the scents of lemon and garlic fill the air. Despite the hostile sounds of the kitchen, it is my favorite place to be. I peer into the various prep stations and pans as the team moves like a ballet company through the steps needed to provide the orders to our diners. The elegance of it excites me and soothes me at the same time.

"Very good. We're on course three for seats five and six, we're on course five for two through four, and our final seating just arrived for seat one. People! Let's go, hustle. I want to go home, and the sooner you have these out the sooner we can get the fuck back to our lives." I clap a few times for emphasis before grabbing the three desserts and heading to the trio of middle-aged women.

They giggle and I do my best to smile and put on the show, despite wanting to be anywhere but here. I've nicknamed them Yakko, Wakko, and Dot like the Animaniacs because there's clearly a sarcastic ringleader, a person who would have preferred a full meal, and the shy one that I'm pretty sure is actually in charge.

"Alright, ladies, it's been a blast but we're on your final plate. For dessert, I've combined a few of my favorite seasonal things. In the bowl you'll find a single scoop of coconut ice cream, topped with candied orange peels dipped in a mixture of milk and dark chocolate. Lastly, on the side is a pistachio shortbread cookie. With Christmas Eve tomorrow, I wanted to include a nod to our name, Sin," I say when I'm cut off.

Purring, Yakko says, "This entire meal has been truly *sinful*," causing cackles to erupt across the group, I look to the side to exhale my irritation and notice the hard eye roll of the blonde in seat one.

"Oh no, looks like we're no longer the best entertainment when there's the young one here," Dot says, correctly clocking me.

Giving a light cough into my elbow to clear my throat I smile wide. "Nonsense, checking to see how the rest of the place is looking. Yes, the goal is for every dish to be sinfully delicious. It also is my goal to fuse the high end with the familiar, and to introduce a few flavors from two of my favorite cuisines. See, I love my grandmother's Persian kitchen, but I also love late-night takeout American style Chinese food."

Despite talking to the trio, my eyes watch seat one, curious to see if there's any flicker of recognition. If she's going to tell me more about her Hamsa or if she'll emphasize it as a hand of Fatima. Her blonde strands and light golden-brown eyes seem mismatched to her skin tone, maybe she's a mix of Ashki and Mizrachi, too?

While my thoughts drift away from the guests I'm expected to focus on, my bar runner brings over a trio of espresso martinis.

"Well, to pair with the items on the plate, here is an orange infused vodka espresso martini. You can drink it alongside or pour over the ice cream to enjoy affogato style. Whatever is your pleasure." I give a wink to seat one who is fully eavesdropping now and the Animaniacs are now hooting and hollering. As I retreat to the kitchen for her first plate, I hear Yakko and Wakko instigating some more. Except this time, they seem to be trying to act as my wing women and I thank my lucky stars for that.

shae

"QUE LINDO," one of the women says as the chef retreats.

"Since when do you speak Spanish, Amy?" one of them asks, the tone heavy with irritation.

"Since we met Michaela's new boyfriend, I've been using one of those app things," Amy says. The trio cackles, and I do my best to not to watch too closely.

But then the sassy one says drunkenly at full volume, "Blondie over here knows what's up. And forget everyone who is here is here for the *am-bee-yance*," really elongating and over emphasizing the word ambiance.

I muffle a laugh into my water glass as I watch the man return to the other group of diners holding their intermezzo. He's more relaxed with this pair than the trio, and I see a bit of his smile. He places the three spoons down, wipes his hands on the bar rag hanging from his apron, and rolls his coat sleeves up. The roped muscles and sinew, the veins, and the light dusting of dark black hair catch my eye.

As he turns his arm, I see his inner wrist has something scrawled there. I knew that Chef Hakimi was known for Sin's fusion menu, which combined his love of Americanized Chinese food with the dishes he grew up on. His tanned brown skin with golden undertones, the mentions of his grandma's Tahdig, and his last name is *Hakimi*. It fits that his father's side is Persian. Getting under this tattooed Taylor Zakhar Perez doppelganger might be the perfect way to spend tonight. He is sinfully handsome; the loud drunken moms next to me are right about that.

"This is a blood-orange and pomegranate sorbet meant to cleanse the palette. It is the perfect balance of flavors in addition to symbolism. You see, the pomegranate is believed all across Asia to represent fertility with the hundreds to thousands of seeds in each ripe fruit. Meanwhile, the color of the flesh and juices of the blood orange have meant to many medieval Europeans strength and power. They are also a symbol of happiness and good fortune. By combining the two, consider this bite a clear pathway to a wonderful meal ahead. Enjoy." He turns to me with a wink before disappearing again.

The bar runner pops by. "On your left," she says before dropping a drink at my side.

Before I can ask about it, she's dipped away. I lift the etched crystal rocks glass and swirl the cocktail, examining the colorful liquid and the floral inclusion.

"A hibiscus flower," the chef says as he places a dish of bread and dips before me. His smile is wide and captivating. His clean-shaven jaw starting to sprout a five o'clock shadow. His dark brown eyes are topped by heavy, expressive eyebrows. He's far less cantankerous with me.

"Specifically, this is a hibiscus mojito to start off with a nod to Little Havana. The lime flavors in the cocktail pair nicely with the garlic-lime hummus and fresh flatbread. Next to it, you'll find a simple spiced virgin olive oil. Completing the trio is a creamy and cheesy artichoke spread. The meal kicks off with something sweet, something sour, something umami, and really wakes up the palate."

The trio of cougars to my side whistle and hoot, giggling as they prepare to leave. The outgoing one says briefly, "Thank your Uncle Eli from us. We'll see him at the next Mahjong tournament, and we expect him to now include that sorbet in the future. Hopefully, you had some so your strong, *fertile* masculinity can work on the blushing blondie."

Oh good lord. I roll my eyes, but before I can reply, they're out the door and cackling.

"Are we all here because of your Uncle Eli?" I ask, grinning at the idea that his uncle is as pushy as my father Gabe.

"Just the four of you, but now that they've left, I can say I am already more optimistic about this extra seat he pilfered than the others," he says. He is grinning wide. Holding up a finger to signal *one moment* he turns and goes back to the kitchen.

I watch him serve the other couple their main course, and disappear once more. This time, returning with a tiny plate of vegetables I hope is for me. "My apologies, but it looks like given Uncle Eli made this reservation after we'd done our weekly orders, there's no more of the Bok choy salad. In its place, can I offer you a custom dish?" He appears to be a mix of annoyed and apologetic, like this is not the experience he wanted to give.

"Sure, what is it?" I ask salivating from the scent of caramelized onions.

"This is a poach pear and brie tart topped with caramelized onions," he says conspiratorially. "This is from a test batch. They're actually Asian Pears. There was a whole thing earlier, I won't bore you. I would love to know what you think. Here, have it with a glass of Sancerre." He places the long-stemmed glass down with a gentle plink.

This time, I'm able to see that his tattoo says *bon appetite* in typewriter font. Giggling, I ask, "A little on the nose isn't it?"

"If you think that's too obvious, you should see some of the others," he quips back.

"Dare I ask?" I say, raising an eyebrow suspiciously.

"I have a butterfly tramp stamp," he deadpans.

"Do you really?" I ask, bewildered by this admission.

He ignores me and gestures to urge me to take a bite. I cut a delicate piece of the poached fruit, cheese, and onion torte. I bring the tines to my mouth and take in the sweet, complex, creamy mix of flavors. My tongue is exploding with each layer of flavor and texture, and I let out a small hum of appreciation.

"Tell me what happened to create this if you don't want to admit you have the tattoo of a spring breaker from your birth year," I say. Lifting the glass, I eye him while pulling in a large sip of the crisp white wine.

"You positive that you want me to go on about produce to you?" he asks, a sweet and shy hesitation despite his flirtatiousness.

"I'm not, but what the hell. We're here," I say and wave a hand around the emptying dining room. "I'm officially on vacation and who doesn't love a good story?"

"Alright, you asked for it... I needed pomegranates for today. They are sometimes called *Chinese Apples*, but *only* in New York or New Jersey. It's a regional thing. My uncle is an investor in Sin and sometimes likes to help." Simon says help with a level of irritation that as the resident 'troubled child' I know too well. I nod enthusiastically as I continue to polish off my glass of wine. While he talks, he opens the bottle and refills my glass.

"Alright so you have my former New Yorker uncle who knows I need pomegranates and looks at the weekly order and sees *Asian Pear* and somehow he decides that *must* be the same as his recollection of *Chinese Apple* on order forms when he first started working up north. So yesterday, my weekly delivery arrived with a huge crate of these *Chinese Apples*, except they were neither apples nor pomegranates. They are a third thing: an Asian fruit that despite its apple shape, is more closely related to a pear." He pauses and watches me carefully.

I'm sipping on the second wine glass, hanging on to his every animated word about fruit and pushy father figures.

"God, this sounds like my dad. Gabe would totally do something like this and then be like"—affecting his mixed Middle Eastern and New Jersey accent—"*Nu*, what? I am *helping*. Ehh." I end on a long note and wave my hands animatedly. He laughs, and as his sleeves move and his neck turns, I notice there are sprinkles of black ink everywhere. Saliva pools in my mouth, I want to peel his chef's coat off and examine every fucking speck of it. With my nails and tongue.

From the appetizer course onward, my meal progresses slowly. More of the standard dining service guests trickle out. The couple on the end have finished their dessert and are headed out with their palms together, fingers interlaced.

With each course my muscles are loosening further, my shoulders unwind and I turn my head slightly to hear a reverberating crack of my neck. "Ah, that's better." I exhale deeply and say to myself quietly.

"What's better, Blondie?" Chef Hakimi asks me as he drops a second dessert at my seat.

If I didn't know any better, I'd think he was trying to keep me here. I drop my elbows onto the countertop. Fortunately for him, I want to be kept. For tonight at least. Leaning forward enough to know the low cut of my top has the perfect amount of cleavage and lace slipping into view. My voice husky, heavy with the feeling that comes with a good meal I say, "Well, first it was that my neck finally cracked. Your uncle really managed to take a rough day and make it worse."

We're interrupted by a team exiting the kitchen and peering around the dining room. Catching my attention, I realize I'm the only customer left. He dismisses and tips out his staff, no more rushed anxiety, just the same boyish grin he wears when telling stories about food.

After their well wishes for the holiday, I nervously ask, "Should I be heading out?"

I don't want to leave, I want to stay in this little bubble of food, flirting, and his story telling forever. I'm no fan of the idea of insta-love, but I'm big on insta-*lust*, and this man is exquisite. His muscular form fills his chef's whites well, his well-groomed and angular face draw me in.

Instinctively I lick my lips as his gaze flicks to my mouth. He's in front of me in two long strides. Pressing my back against the counter I've been seated at, he looms over me. Like the women of my family, I'm small, not clearing more than five feet and change. He's likely no more than five foot ten, but that's enough to dwarf me. His eyes flick from mine to my lips and back again. My lips part and my breath slowly exhales. It's both immediate and ages between that exhale and his mouth finding mine.

Permission is granted using body language. I push up on my toes in my high heels trying to reach him better. His head dips lower, our kiss connects and immediately, there is a hunger that consumes me. Every movement is impassioned with this handsome near-stranger.

Tongues part lips, we lick in and out of each other's mouths, then it's a wrestling match for the lead. His teeth find my lower lip softly as his hands explore up and down the length of my ribs and back.

The openness of the dress leaves much of my skin exposed to his and his touch ignites everything inside me that has been pent up. *Thank god* his guttural noises are carnal. Somewhere in the back of my thoughts are the insecurities I have over my recent stress-induced weight loss. The long hours at work have me on a diet of coffee and power bars too often.

On some lonely late nights, before I get to swiping and find myself a partner for release, I've questioned if it has changed my prospects. When he squeezes my ass, strong hands using firm pressure, I let go of any insecurity. The thoughts float away with the moan that crawls through my entire being and escapes from deep in my throat.

"She likes that huh," he rasps before squeezing me once more, harder this time.

I lean into his touch, moaning again. Pulling back to meet his eyes, he pauses and gazes down at me. He's studying my necklace, my Hamsa necklace, the hand for protection. I reach for it and wrap a finger around the delicate gold symbol and wait.

"You need to tell me your name, Blondie," he says this while holding our hips firm against one another.

Holding me against him this way presses his hardening cock against my hip, making his manhood known despite the layers of fabric separating us. My pulse quickens and feels like the thunderous noise of a horse race kicking off. The offbeat, constant pounding of my core increasing the ache. I need to be touched, I need to release the stress and pressure.

"*Blondie*, huh? Does that make you a brownie?" I ask giggling over my terrible joke.

"You want to be dessert?" he says, his eyes blackening and his face assessing. Checking for permission. Checking that he isn't misreading this.

I like that. I like watching as he waits for my signal.

Gripping my ass firmly, he lifts me onto the counter and slides his hands up and down my thighs.

"I'm on the pill, I get tested between partners, and I prefer you use a condom," I say and place my hand on the thin strap of my dress. Slowly lowering the string and letting it and the top of my dress fall to the side exposing my breast and the barbell in my nipple.

He swallows and I watch the muscles of his neck working. "I'm, uh, clean? No. That's not how I'm supposed to say it anymore. I'm good? That's too vague. I…" He runs a hand through his hair, slicking it back from his face.

Enjoying how flustered he is, I cup my breast and massage. "Medically in the clear for this?" I supply, hoping he will understand that I got the point.

"Yes, that. I..." He's about to go way deeper than I'm prepared for, emotionally.

I wave a hand to cut him off. "No more talking, show me what that mouth can do other than tell stories."

He wasn't prepared like I was because this is my goal tonight—a casual encounter with a beautiful stranger. After this dinner, I'm going to go dancing. Once inside a night club, sweaty and pressed together, I'll find someone to slip away with. I didn't want anything to delay getting mine and going home, so he's in for a treat when he finally— "Oh," I gasp, his hands firmly pulling my thighs apart cutting off my thoughts.

"If you eat half as well as you cook, it would be impossible to turn down," I say, giving a smirk and raking my nails through the hairs at the nape of his neck.

He licks his lips, blackened eyes staring at my exposed pussy damp with arousal.

"Actually," he says with a diabolical glint to his eyes, "I'm proud to say that I eat twice as well as I cook." Then he moves his hand right where I'm aching for him most. "And you are so wet for me baby, aren't you?"

"God, yes," I cry as he teases me with his large, calloused fingers between my leg and my pussy. My outer lips. He continues to bring his hands back down my thigh and a bit closer with each pass before I give a groan of frustration. "I. Don't. Believe. You," I manage to pant out, trying to goad him into finally fucking touching me.

He's right there, millimeters from where I'm dripping for him, and he leans in. On a whisper he says, "Liar," at the same moment he plunges two fingers deep inside me. His other hand shifts my skirt up higher, the cold marble against my skin. Lowering himself so his lips meet my aching core, he pulls my clit into his mouth. I cease thinking as my body reacts by dripping further onto his chin.

"Oh Blondie, you taste so sweet," he says while pumping his

fingers in and out of me. Shifting to adjust so I'm across the counter and he's leaning forward, face pressed to the most sensitive parts of me.

"Damn right," I grunt while tightening my hold on his nape.

"Fuck yes, ride my face, let's go," he says with an exuberance that adds to the building tension in my body.

He follows my lead as I press him toward my writhing hips. His tongue parts my lips and licks a long line to the underside of my clit. His breath, hot and warm, caresses my throbbing nerve endings before he pulls my clit between his lips and sucks slow and hard.

"Harder," I beg. His mouth tightens around me and my knees fall to his ears.

He eagerly hums his appreciation, I feel the tense rise, my core is clenching around his fingers. I need more, I want to feel stretched to my limits. I'm trying to tell him but I'm panting through my words.

"One." *Breath.* "Add one." *Pant.* "More," I finally get out fragmented. Instead of adding one more finger right away, he pulls his hand back and now I'm clenching around nothing. Desperate for release, yet so fucking close.

He runs his slick fingers on my bare thigh, mixing his saliva with my arousal. I watch as he grabs my discarded water glass from dinner and fishes inside, pulling out a small piece of ice. Our eyes meet and he cocks a brow, silently asking for permission. I release a primal moan, forceful, like no sound I've heard myself ever make. Taking the sliver of cold between his lips, he presses three fingers inside me before adding the cold of his lips into the mix. With that, I am quickly thrust into depths of the ocean, everything is cold and hot at once. Wet. It is so wet.

Did I knock over the glass or did I come all over us? Who fucking cares?

I'm shaking and squeezing my thighs for control but it's all gone. My body is calling the shots and she's fucking elated. "Oh. My. God." I shout, followed by more nonsensical words.

He stills his hand deep inside me, curling his fingers just so until he hits a deep pleasure zone and everything is warm and slick. Definitely coming. Thank fuck. My body slows, my breathing heavy and languid, until I'm half-lidded and peering down at this handsome stranger.

I'm planning to fix my skirt, thank him for dinner and the entertainment, and make a hasty exit. Except, he stands and licks his hand clean and stares at me.

Ohh baby. Mama like, a voice in my head purrs. Both of us panting out of sync and locked in a staring contest, I look for the break to exit. "That was fucking phenomenal, I could use a cigarette," I say and hop down.

"Then you're in luck. Um, also, don't worry. I'm not expecting anything in return. I'm sure after being in the kitchen all night—" He scratches at the back of his head a bit weary. "Whatever, let's pop out into the alley, come on." Holding out his hand, Chef Hakimi guides me through the prep kitchen to the service entrance.

Propping the door open with a lone brick, he digs through the pockets of his coat and pants before producing a small cardboard box. I was mostly kidding, but honestly a cigarette sounds right. I wouldn't consider myself much more than a social smoker but get enough cocktails in me and the crowd heads outside—I'm going to join them. With the white stick dangling from his lip, he finds a tiny matchbox and lights his.

The deep inhale and exhale he takes feels sensual. He leans in so I can light the end of my own from his, holding my eyes and puffing slowly to ensure the embers catch. Why is this so fucking hot despite all the reasons I know it shouldn't be? Hot damn.

"So Blondie, you planning to tell me your name? Or is this it. You eat the best meal of your life, get eaten by the best you'll ever have, steal one of my cigs and disappear as the sweetest mystery dessert?" he asks, his tone laced with mischief.

"Maybe," I say. I take a drag and let my eyes rove over him as he undoes the white coat fully. My gaze lands on the hideous neon plastic clogs and I exhale on a laugh. "Oh, my god. What is on your feet?" My laughter growing to howls.

"Shut up, they're comfortable for work. I got this color for Miami," he replies, pointing a toe like he's showing off the shoe despite sounding a bit peeved.

simon

BUMPING HER SANDAL with my *ugly plastic neon clogs*, I ask again, "Well? What will it be?"

"Does it matter?" she asks in a husky voice exhaling my direction.

"Is this where tonight turns into a true crime podcast?" I ask. Clasping my hands together, I drop onto one knee. "Please, oh please, I'm too young to die," I coo and try to force my face into an innocent doe-eyed look.

The lit cigarette in her hand dangles low enough to be a little dangerous. I question if this was a horrible idea. She flicks the ash into the wind so it flies in my direction. Then she laughs and lightly pushes my forehead with her open palm. I exaggerate wobbling my head back, snapping forward with a full-beam smile and our laughs meld together. It feels like watching sugar melt in the pan and swirl from grainy to a soft, creamy, drizzled sauce. It feels like that first amazing bite of seasonal fruit. It was really fucking good sex and my dick wasn't even in her yet.

"I think Blondie works just fine." She laughs around the final drag on her cigarette. Grabbing the stub from her hand to make sure to snuff the remaining embers on the designated brick and drop the butt into the coffee can ashtray.

"Blondie, I know you know my name. Seems unfair." I lean in, pressing my mouth to her neck and sucking on the pulse point. I lightly nip and hear a hard smack on my chest. When the pain registers, I step back with hands raised and feeling sheepish. "Sorry, too far?"

Her eyes narrow, causing her nose to scrunch ever so slightly. I'm expecting her to storm off. I'm expecting a takedown of epic proportions as her eyes blacken fully eliminating all of the mischief there before. From her hardened gaze, she sharply asks, "Do you really have a butterfly tramp stamp?"

I choke on my exhale, and steel myself into a mirror of her no bullshit stare to better lean into the standoff. I angle my body ever so slightly forward and slowly lower my hands. Allowing my eyes to run up and down her frame and trying to keep them as focused points isn't easy, but I give this my all.

The static charge is heavier than the humidity, weighing on us and crackling through the air. Nodding once, purposefully, I say, "Wouldn't you like to know." Neither of us can contain it any longer and we dissolve into laughter.

The laugh ends abruptly from Blondie and she repeats herself, "But do you?"

I freeze, unsure if this is the same joke. She looks sweet but sounds like she might actually be able to harm me. "Um," I say in an effort to buy time. "So, I have a lot of tattoos all over," I hedge, unsure what to say.

The crackling sensation is back, and with the increased charge in the air I jump with a shriek like I've never seen lightning or heard a loud thunderclap before. Blondie's laugh returns, brighter than before. She throws her head back in the enjoyment and it reminds me how she looked a few minutes before, breathy and euphoric.

"I have a proposition for you, Brownie," she says. Her body still angled slightly toward mine, she licks her lips carefully.

Swallowing thickly, I widen my stance. I may only be 5'10", but I hold a physical advantage. Unless she has a weapon. *Do you think she would have a weapon? She looks like a Girl Scout! No, Blondie here wouldn't. She couldn't.* I'm so fucked, I can't decide what I believe.

Crossing my arms over my chest, I harden my gaze and force my muscles to relax. The Mystery Dessert doesn't need to know her cagey behavior has me on alert when it isn't so adorable I have to laugh. A curt nod is all I give in reply.

"I have been trying to figure out from your stories, your food, if you have somewhere to be tomorrow or..." she trails off. Maybe I'm not the only one who is starting to question being alone, in an alley, late at night with a stranger.

Curious how she's going to play this out, I hold my stance and wait her out. "Or..." I prod her to continue.

Sharp tongued and quick on her feet though, she immediately snaps back into the previous confident display. "Or, are you also free for the next two days, like me?" Her voice is strong, no bullshit. Her body is controlled and relaxed.

Struggling to hide the uncertainty lingering under the surface as I run through worst case scenarios, I question out loud, "Are you a honey trap sent to take me?"

Her lips twitch and she bites down to hold in a smirk, but the tone of her voice is all play. "Who told you?"

"I was just going to suggest you shower and hit the town with me, as long as you don't have some sort of Christmas family thing to do tomorrow. I want to see all that Miami has to offer while my office is closed. You seem like you'd be able to make anywhere fun," she says shrugging.

Wrapping one arm around her shoulders and exaggeratedly smelling the opposite underarm with a noisy inhale, I turn and guide her. Opening the door, I wave one hand to say *after you* with a slight nod inside. "After you, party girl," I tease.

32

Inside, I grab my duffle, keys, and phone from the office. Walking back toward her with phone in hand I quickly scroll through the texts from industry friends wishing me a Merry Christmas Eve, calling out where they are hanging out post-closing. Last, there is one from Uncle Eli asking if I "smoothed things over for blondie from Shine," giving me a little more information than before. I toss that text a thumbs up, shove my phone into the pocket of my pants.

"I can definitely do that, Blondie from Shine," I say giving a wink. Flipping the light switch, the building is now cloaked in darkness save for the glow of a few emergency exit signs. Slinging the duffle over my shoulder, I wave my keys and ask, "Did you have a place in mind for this shower? My place or yours?"

"I have a hotel room in South Beach, my friend is trying to confirm that I'm on the list for the club she was obsessed with before moving to Philly," she says, pulling her phone from her bag and scrolling her notifications up and down without deleting them. Animal.

"Oh god, not that college spot. The boat shoe place?" I groan. She does look preppy enough for that horrible spot to spend daddy's money.

"You mean Chukker? Oh, god no. I had my fill of that place when I had a fake ID years ago. Gross." She shudders.

"Do you mean one of those overpriced, velvet rope, types of places?" I ask and quirk a brow continuing to guide her to my car. In full view under the streetlight is my baby, a sporty coupe with a paint job that matches my *ugly clogs*.

Giving a low whistle, she smiles from ear to ear.

"You a car girl?" I ask pushing the button to unlock the doors.

She opens the passenger side and slides in like this is totally normal. She's wild.

"Not even a little bit, but this looks like it will go *zoom*," she squeals and claps her hands.

I slide in behind the steering wheel, pass her my phone and ask her to punch in which hotel for the GPS. Reaching the highway entrance, I hit the gas and let it rip. She's cheering and giggling.

"Woohoo!" she shouts toward the night sky. "Take that, fuckers!"

Joy radiates off her and despite the wind whipping between us in my convertible, I feel a sense of warmth and belonging. I let a low wolf whistle out, joining her in this celebration of something.

I pull up to the valet and let them know it won't be long and trail Blondie into the lobby. I follow her to the elevator bank and wait while she pushes the button.

We step into the elevator, and I watch as she uses the keycard to input the floor.

"Seriously, am I going to call you Blondie all night?" I ask again.

"What do you want to call me?" she teases over her shoulder.

"At this point, Chukker, since I'm not convinced we aren't going there," I say making a silly face. I know when she looks in the mirrored wall she will see it.

When she finally does, it causes her it huff out a small laugh.

"If I'm Chukker, then you'd be Miami Ink," she teases.

"Wait, you know my cousin?" I ask deadpan.

"What?" she stammers, turns, and paces the few square feet of the elevator.

On her next pass, I put out an arm to stop her.

"Red rover, red rover, send Blondie on over," I tease and wrap my arms around her.

The elevator dings and she is still looking a bit dazed, so I place one hand over the frame to keep the doors from closing. "This is you, yeah?" I ask, placing a palm on the small of her back and guiding her out.

"Yes. Wait, but seriously, are you related to someone from Miami Ink?" she asks, still a bit bewildered. She blinks once, shakes her hair out, and seems to have reset.

"I can't tell where the joke ends and the truth begins," she admits and then rushes to cover that with more details. "Also, I haven't had a break in fucking forever. I am looking forward to tonight, now I'm trying to figure out what else is open over Christmas Eve and Christmas. Otherwise, I'm going to be a lonely Jew on Christmas." She pouts as she waves her hand to follow as we walk by the identical doors with large gold numbers on them.

Reaching the end of the hallway, she presses the keycard to the reader. The little lights turn green and blink before the mechanical gears move and click into place signaling the door is unlocked.

"Standard hotel suite, bathroom has all the things you could need. It's over there." She points and takes her shoes off before plopping down on top of the king-size bed. "I'm going to power nap, wake me when you are ready to go. And don't rob me, Chef, or I'll use the power of the press release and end you."

I'm about to rebuff, but her eyes close and the sounds of soft even breathing are nearly immediate. Damn.

shae

I'M NOT ASLEEP; that would be ridiculous. I need to make some quick decisions and that was an easy way to end the conversation. Once I hear the bathroom door click, I quickly roll over and grab my phone.

Shae: Girl. Am. I. In? Hello?

Shae: Seriously, it's been hours.

Shae: The fuck? Don't ask me to fix your ugly ass presentations if you can't reply.

Shae: SARAH?

Fuck, I groan to myself. I know I found a guy, so in theory I could stay in and roll around. Except, I need more. I need to breathe in the life of this town.

I want to drink. Meander under the streetlights and make friends out of strangers. Those friends meaning we land in the backyard of their friends, until a new adventure is born. I want to eat from the spot that is too good to be that cheap. The kind only locals know about.

I want to make memories that are worth telling stories about. If I ever have kids, I want their kids to laugh and say *ew, grandma you were wild.* Then secretly, the wild one will know they can come to me. I want to live so that when I look back on my life, I'm not so bored I want to die. I want to quietly tell these to my siblings' kids when they're older so the wild one knows I'm their ally.

My older sister, Nessa, has a fucking doctorate from Harvard. She's always got it all together, and now she's landed herself a rich, handsome, and *fun* partner in Mateo. Tal is still in school, but they are set to get a bachelors and masters combined in five years. They have all this leadership stuff and plans for working to keep advocating for the queer community, my lawyer parents love it. Then, the baby. Joshua is a senior in high school and decided recently he wants to become a veterinarian. He got into an ivy just like *perfect Nessa*. Everyone is so smart, they are so serious, they don't understand me.

ALL SIBS CHAT [NESSA, Mateo, Shae, Tal, and Shua]

Shea: How's Nessa's first official Christmas with Matty's family going?

Nessa: Last year was the first one, you were there.

Shae: Nah.

Tal: Yeah, we didn't do the Filipino traditions. You're going to midnight mass soon.

Shae: SHUT UP, you're going to church? Does Ema know?

Nessa: Mom knows.

Shae: Am I not the scandal for once?

Nessa: Depends, where are your panties?

Tal: Does Shae wear panties?

Shae: Not tonight… and my new friend turned off the shower, so I gotta run. And this is the sibling chat WITH Shua, so let's not discuss my panties here again. K? Merry Christmas, Nessa Santos-Manolo!

Nessa: I'm not engaged, don't do that.

Shua Rabin: I'm 17 & ur gross

. . .

I DROP my phone and flip onto my stomach too fast. It's a poor attempt to fake still napping. A cool, rough palm skims the back of my legs to the top of my skirt then disappears. Not more than a few moments later, there's a loud pop! The sting from his smack on my ass causes me to exhale. I think we both can hear that it doesn't sound pained, but wildly turned on.

Immediately, that hand is back on my skin, rubbing in a soothing pattern.

"Finding you ass up like this, it was too tempting," he says, words laced with heat.

"Fuck," I groan and lift one eyelid.

Water sluices down his inked frame and ends at the white towel wrapped around his hips, his leanly muscled body on display. Down his ribs is painted the most intricate Hamsa, with tiny details including the pomegranates he served in many ways tonight. *Mmm, yum.*

"You like that, Shae?" he says, pronouncing my name like the adjective 'shy.'

Instinctively I correct him. "Shae, like where the Mets play." *Fuck.*

"Well, *Shae where the Mets Play*, I'm Simon. But you knew that. Or *Shimon the Rimon* if you're my mom. Hence the..." he mimics me then waves his hand over the pomegranate tattoo.

I push myself up onto my elbows and look around trying to figure out where he found my name. That's when the scrolling words on the television catch my eye.

"Crap. I forgot hotel TVs are all tech-savvy and personalized now," I whine.

"So slugger, you a baseball fan?" he asks while digging around his bag.

I groan and roll my eyes ending that conversation.

Simon drops the towel and hot damn! I'll take what he's

working with, thanks. The dark hair on his chest thins into a soft line curving around his belly button and thickening again down his abdomen. He must feel my eyes on him, because Simon flexes his stomach then hops into a pair of jeans sans boxers, and palms his impressive length and adjusts its position. His outstretched fingers move along the five-button fly with ease, deftly cinching and maneuvering.

He lifts the leather duffle, digging around again and pulling out a little ruby red velvet bag. He gently shakes it and produces a gold rope chain. The clasp secured, it drops along his collar bone and I'm tempted to yank him by it into this bed with me.

His low-slung jeans show off the bronzed skin and black inked chest, arms, and ribs like a spotlight. He is covered in symbols, foods, utensils, and words. The entire body a canvas retelling his story.

He pulls out a handful of products, a brush, and a black shirt. Turning to the mirror, I see the full expanse of his back. A lion with a wild mane stares at me, and the excitement in my pulse hits again. Everywhere. "We could stay in," I muse.

Simon turns and closes the distance between us. "I assumed you said all that to get me up here in bed with you, Blondie." He drags a finger down my nose and ends with a light tap.

I tilt my head, contemplating what to say next. I'm trying to explain this idea I have, but I'm still not sure. On the one hand, I'd like to invite him to spend Christmas with me doing anything we can find open over Christmas. On the other hand, we've known each other for a few hours. Before I can find the *right* way to propose my plan he jumps in.

"Am I about to pass out and wake up in that tub full of ice? Shit. I knew it was too good to think this was okay. You don't want my kidneys, I swear." He seems genuinely freaked out at first, but the twitch near his mouth tells me he's got jokes.

"I'm more interested in seeing Miami and getting laid. Plus, I'm not great with a bone saw. I was thinking." I give a low hum and blurt out the truth, "Honestly? I'm tired of being forced into the same annual arguments. Spoiler alert: the baby of the family will pick our movie, we *will* order a Peking Duck. We'll have a proper American *Jewish Christmas* and I'll be bored. I've been working too hard; I want to have fun. So I'm here to work, but this is my chance to live."

He turns and leans against the dresser, his back on display in the mirror, his eyes locked with mine. I move to sit up on my knees and feel the strap of my dress falling. I leave it, letting the way I'm imperfect and undone and willing to go on a messy adventure shine.

His cock thickens and presses against the button fly. *Doesn't that hurt?*

His hand on his chin, skimming the five o'clock shadow, I watch him contemplate.

"Please, will you have a Christmas adventure with me, Simon? If it's open, I want to check it out. If it's delicious, I want two of them. I want to be free; I want to relax. I want to do something that will be a story worth telling my grandkids with someday. You in?"

"Aw, Blondie, thank you so much for not expecting me to father your kids but be a wild story you remember. It's like you get me," Simon says with a hand over his heart, his pec flexing, but a pinch of irritation laced behind his eyes.

"You would rather I was looking for you to propose?" I toss back and he makes the most adorable face as he contemplates what to say.

"How about we get those drinks first. Fuck some more, then we can shop for an engagement ring after Christmas if all goes well."

simon

"I DOUBT you'll still be thinking that when I'm done with you," I say then pull my black V-neck overhead.

"Bet?" Her mouth slowly breaks into a wide smile. A shimmer behind her eyes hints at something I want to lean in toward, like following the white light.

"Bet," I confirm with a solemn nod. I don't think that I'm going to forget whatever this is anytime soon, and certainly not the next day. Even if I *also* don't expect to want to marry her.

"Hmm, okay so we have a deal. By the time the clock strikes midnight welcoming December twenty-sixth we'll part ways. I'll have a fantastic story and you'll be off shopping for engagement rings for a woman you'll never be able to find again," she muses, one delicate blush pink fingernail tracing her lips.

"Yep," I say, repeating the nod.

"Yep." She nods in return.

Holding out a hand, palm up, I offer to assist as she gets out of bed, the plush mattress and boxspring placing the pixie sized woman so far from the ground. Her tiny, soft hand has long delicate fingers. Everything about her looks so sweet and slight, young. Not *so young* that it feels illegal, yet when her honey brown eyes flick upward, she looks innocent. Maybe it's the doe-eyes, because despite her innocent stare, she's formidable as she hops off the bed ignoring my hand.

Definitely the tougher one of us. She looks sweet but might be able to kill me, I look like I could kill but I'm too soft for that. Sounds like something in one of my sisters' romance novels. The thought of my sister snaps me back to the present and I feel compelled to check in.

"Okay... all jokes aside. I'm a strange man; you're alone in a new city. Who knows where you are? About me?" I ask, picking up her phone and passing it her way.

"Okay, *Daddy*, my big sister has us all on some app to know everything we do. I'm pretty sure she gave me a microchip in my sleep. It may collect health data too." The eye roll and crossed arms during the scoff were adorable. "Does that work for you, *Daddy?*" she says, repeating the term and I'm struck by the way my dick twitches along with her sultry question.

I clear my throat and shift my stance. "Don't call me that, and good. I'm on my way to celebrity status, sweetheart, can't have you sully my pristine reputation."

The tiniest hint of a laugh escapes before she pulls her lips in to swallow the sound.

This is going to be fun.

"We wouldn't want to sully your virtue, I mean... *reputation*," she says, the ghost of a smile back on her lips.

"I'm a *very* virtuous man; I appreciate that you've got my back. You know how it is for us mid-profile celebrities. Not big enough to hire the likes of Shine, but not small enough to not think about a local headline or two," I say, realizing the playful statement has veered off course into honest territory.

Shae walks across the room where a suitcase is propped up on one of those fold out holders and bends over far enough to show off the curve of ass cheek at the hem of her dress. She digs around a bit and pulls forward a zipped case. I watch enraptured as she opens it, pulls out a beautiful pair of Nike Air Jordan's in metallic gold and ankle socks. She covers her bare feet and says, "You promised me dancing. You ready?"

I throw my hips in a series of salsa moves and singsong in time to my reply, "It's a good thing my plans start with heading to Havana. Ready, Blondie?"

"In Cuba? I didn't pack a passport," she asks.

Her top teeth dip into the pillow of her lower lip, she pauses. The stillness is broken by a dip of her brow, face tensing with growing confusion.

"Little Havana is a neighborhood, and my buddies have a table at our favorite spot that will feed us after we close," I say trying to catch her up to speed, and hoping the way I was stepping and wiggling my hips will connect.

Shae twirls and her skirt bounces and confirms she never put on underwear. My hand skims along the smooth silk of the dress and tease just under the hemline. My hand grazes along her hip, and I yank her close. Close enough to feel the way she's caused my cock to get heavy as he pulses and jumps. "You've woken up the Macabee, Blondie. That isn't a hammer in my pants, although I am *very* happy to see you don't wear underwear ever."

I feel her head press into my chest, the softness of her ponytail swishing against my arm, she smells sweet and salty. I try to see her face and catch a tinge of pink on her swollen cheeks. The chuckle pushes past her pressed lips, and she peers up through her lashes.

"Oh god, I can't believe I was going to suggest staying back and taking care of that, but—" she expels another fluttering lipped giggle. "But you called your dick your *Macabee Soldier*?"

The laughs continue to grow, and I give myself an eight-count to drink her in. The way her apple cheeks grow puffier, the scrunch of her nose, the shake of her body pressed to mine. Threading her ponytail around my wrist, I yank hard enough to force our eyes to meet and stay there. The hold strong enough to elicit a soft exhale and her pupils turn into pools of espresso, all other color banished.

"You trying to stay in? Or would you rather go dancing and get finger fucked all over the city?" I ask, my voice deep and commanding.

I loosen my grip enough to allow her neck to nod ever so slightly. She's panting, tense everywhere, waiting. Finally, she whispers, "You into that?"

Tension coils around us, debauchery and decadence swirling. While her eyes sparkle and dare me to call it a bluff, they seem to silently beg with intense desire. Slowly at first, the room warms until the feeling accelerates and tops out. A simple "I'm not *not* into that" is the most I can say. Our bodies pressed close, so ready to say fuck it and throw her onto the hotel bed.

While lost in my thoughts and trying to decide what I wanted more, Shae loosened her hair from my fist and opened the hallway door. "Good, then you have places to be and I'm tagging along."

In a complete daze, I float into the hallway and hear the loud metallic clang of the door closing behind us. Shaking my head I break out of the fog she left me in.

shea

PULLING off the highway into a gas station, Simon parks by a mini-mart and cuts the engine. I look around, and while it's a bit busier than I'd expect for midnight going into December twenty-fourth, it's also pretty underwhelming.

"Kind of basic. Forties in a parking lot?" I say before pressing my head against the soft leather of his seat. Taking a cleansing breath, I turn and find Simon staring at me.

His deep brown eyes look like pools of black ink in the dim light of the parking lot. It has only been a few hours, but there's something familiar there. Whether it's his knowing gaze or the excitement radiating off him, I give in. With a halfhearted shrug and an intentionally exaggerated sigh, I say, "Okay, forties it is."

He stands up and begins to disappear into the dark. I rush to get up and join him. As my hand reaches the lever, however, the door flies open. I gasp, taken by surprise when he is standing there.

Palm extended to me, I sit stunned. His long arm, dusted with deep brown-black hair and tiny pictures in colorful ink, glides across my midsection. With the precision of someone who spent hours learning to use his hands to mold and shape food to his will, he's commanding. First the click of the latch detaching, then a soft touch that lingers across my belly as he makes sure it doesn't snap back. With our bodies pressed this way, his lips easily find the pulse where my jaw meets my neck. Below my ear. He presses a gentle kiss there, then pulls the lobe between his teeth. Exhaling, he releases the skin and whispers, "Shh, secret bar with the best Cuban food in the state."

As quickly as he was there, warm and sensual, he's back to standing in the dim parking lot. I toss my bag over my shoulder and this time, I grab his extended palm. Swiveling my knees together toward the door and dropping my sneakers to the pavement, I exit without incident.

Palms pressed, we walk together through the lot and up to the tiny blue-gray cement building. He releases my hand to open the door, then presses that palm on my low back where the dress leaves my skin uncovered. We walk past the rows of what at first appears to be the usual rest stop goods. Long glass front refrigerators with shiny metallic handles overflowing with water, sports drinks, and sodas. An aisle of gummy candy on one side and chocolate on the other. Yet, on closer examination of the labels, nothing is familiar.

I hear the faintest sound of drums and something higher pitched. The sound reminds me of the bouncy click-clack of heels on tile. I reach the wall of beverages and am about to teasingly ask which can of beer I'm supposed to get for Simon, when I notice these are heavily frosted. Standing there, I lean left, right, bounce on my toes, but I cannot see anything in the case. Yet, when I put my hand on the door, it's warm to the touch. Not dangerously warm, but mismatched to the frozen appearance.

Simon is standing with the clerk, one arm on the high counter, he's slouched over and whispering. They give a masculine but familiar greeting, and whatever is said causes a laugh to burst from the gregarious man behind the counter.

"Do you want anything, Blondie?" Simon calls to me.

"I'd love a forty, since we're in a parking lot. Can't tell what they have though, you?" I reply. I pop a hand on my hip and shake the long ponytail from my shoulder. "Are you more of a high or low brow beer drinker?" I push my hip out a little further, pursing my lips, and take a long look at him. I want him to feel as though he's being deeply examined.

Despite my best attempts at intimidation, the men laugh again.

"Give it a pull, *flaca*, it's fine," the man behind the counter calls.

I try, yanking the warm handle and nothing happens. It doesn't budge slightly.

"Maybe you need to try the one next to it?" Simon offers, though the shit eating grin tells me not to bother.

"Maybe you can help me, since I'm just a girl?" I suggest. I pull my hands low in front of me, clasped like I'm just an innocent baby and flutter my lashes.

Simon turns to his friend and says, "Is Oscar on the clave tonight?"

"You know it my man, have fun." They exchange another handshake when the frosted glass begins to light up in a rotating array of colors. As Simon walks over to me, the man calls out, "And Si." He says it like it rhymes with eye. "Make sure she tries el lechon asado and the *tostones*, need to get some meat on those bones. Mi corazon made them today."

Grasping his heart, Simon turns and says, "Adriana cooked? How did I get so lucky?"

"You're telling me, I ask her that every night. Have fun kids. Feliz Navidad!"

Before I can ask what's happening, the formerly locked door swings inward and exposes a dark hallway. The flashing lights of a club and the sounds of Caribbean music swirl overhead. A banner of Cuban flags wraps around a hostess stand, where a beautiful brunette lights up as we approach.

"Ahh now the party starts, *hola hermano*. Who is this with you tonight?" she asks brightly. She grabs Simon and kisses his cheek.

"Blondie, meet my sister from another mister, Rosa. Rosa, meet Blondie," he says ping ponging his face between us.

"Your usuals?" she asks looking at Simon in a way that causes a twinge of possessiveness to take over. I am standing right here, after all.

"What's the usual, Brownie?" I ask, ignoring Rosa while trying to seem indifferent.

"The corner booth, a truck load of food when Adriana is the one who cooked, and is that Javi at the bar?" Simon asks turning to Rosa.

"You know he doesn't let me host if he isn't anymore," she says laying a hand over her belly, a glint from a diamond ring catching on the blinking strobe. Oops.

We weave through a crowded dance floor and the music reverberates through me. I can feel my bones shaking in time with the band. It makes me feel alive. I don't want to sit and eat; I want to move.

I yank Simon and turn him around, and shout to him over the music, "Dance with me?"

"Rosa, tell Adri I will take anything she wants me to from the kitchen but that Eddie said flaca has to try the lechon and tostones," he calls to the other woman and then turns and wraps a hand around my waist. Our connected palms rise and we begin to step together in time with the rhythm. Our hips nestled close together, my foot moving back in perfect sync with his step forward. While I don't know the song, it seems he must because at one moment he releases me and twirls me away only to bring me back in. This time closer, my back pressed to his front, and the beat speeds up. Shifts to something that remixes tradition and modernity.

We stay that way for the next few songs, moving together and apart like magnets. I've worked up another appetite, and am starting to feel warm when a man in a neon shirt passes holding a large tray.

Hoisted overhead, I see multiple baskets and can smell the scent of fried goodness. Inhaling deeply the food mixes with the masculine scent of Simon and I'd swear I was drunk if I didn't know better. I haven't drank in hours though. This is a different type of buzz. The effervescent kind that I can't get without the hum of people around me.

"What smells so good?" I ask, eyes following the neon shirt like a homing device attached directly to my stomach.

"That would be freshly fried tostones, a smashed and salted root vegetable. Popular throughout the Caribbean. Come on, let's eat," he says and guides me to the table.

Rosa is sitting with her feet propped up on a second chair on one side of the booth. Her heels are beautiful, but they would be painful under normal circumstances. With the swell of her foot, I feel bad I had any uncharitable thoughts. Instead of apologizing, I recall what Emily says in the Emily Shine Method: *e, easy, s, strategic, and m, motivating.* An easy, motivating, strategy? Make his friend more comfortable.

"Hey Rosa, can I grab anything for you before we sit?" I ask.

At the same time, Javi comes over from the bar with a small tray of high ball glasses. "Mojitos all around." Then he drops a kiss on Rosa's lips and says, "A virgin for my girls. A hint of ginger, so hopefully mija will go easier on her mama."

"Thank you, baby," she says with a soft touch. He hops over her and sits at the table at her side. We slide into the booth and hunker down to eat and drink while the musicians play.

The room is still busy, but everyone here looks at home. I soak it in, the lights, the photos, the band comprised of middle-aged men in short sleeved linen button downs. I can't help but tap my fingers along with the beat and slowly pick at bites of everything. I had so much earlier for dinner, but all of this smells amazing.

"You should have seen the night we had Adri try to teach your man here to make her *mojo* so he could add it to the menu." Javi laughs.

"It was fine," Simon says shrugging one shoulder. The hint of a grimace quickly washed away by his sip of the drink. He leans forward, joining in the animated retelling.

"Fine my ass. You asked more questions about a four-ingredient marinade than any human should ever be allowed to ask!" Rosa teases, backing up Javi's claim.

"Yeah, yeah, I wanted to know if it's usually made with sour oranges and limes would it be a *mojo* still if I made it using any of the literal thousand other citrus fruits. What if I did a lemon mix? Would it still be a mojo? What if I picked up Meyer Lemons? Or does the sweetness mean it's no longer close enough to the original to be based on a mojo? What if I used key limes? An etrog?" He's growing more animated with each fruit he lists.

When he says etrog, I nearly do a spit take. The long, bumpy, yellow fruit is common during a fall Jewish holiday, but I've never seen anyone eat or cook with one.

"Here we go again," Javi says with an exaggerated sigh. He cocks his head to the side and then looks directly at me. "You sure you don't want me to introduce you to someone better, flaca? You aren't stuck with him you know."

"Oh I know," I say, smiling and looking around conspiratorially. "I picked him up tonight at dinner, I won't even tell him how to find me later. I needed a tour guide who would be free over Christmas." I give Simon a wink to signal the playfulness of my words.

"Is that so?" Simon pushes back on my claim. We're sitting close, his arm draped across the booth and over my shoulders. Tracing lightly down my arm, he tickles me ever so slowly and gently. Without warning, he presses his fingers into my ribs and tickles me.

I squirm, shrieking with laughter. Pushing gently, I command him, "Stop it," but at the same time, I lean in closer, my nose and his rubbing together. "Otherwise, I have creative ways to get back at you." I trace a flirty line of my own, this one beneath the table.

Rosa rolls her eyes before giving an oversized yawn. "I don't need to be here for this foreplay, can we go crash, mi amor?" She drops her feet from the chair they hung over and rises.

"Whatever my baby wants, my baby gets," Javi says following her lead.

"Nice to meet you, Blondie with no name," Javi adds to me with a wolfish grin. "You enjoy our city. Make sure he shows you his cock."

I can hear Javi and Rosa laughing over the music as they head back into the thick crowd.

"What did he just say?" I ask, concerned I misunderstood. Concerned I understood clearly. What an odd thing to say.

simon

"HE SAID to show you my cock," I reply, giving her a grin.

I know the way it sounds, but if how our night began is a sign, Shae isn't prudish. Her double take betrays her surprise, but there's heat behind her eyes.

"Whip it out then, big boy," she says teasing my denim covered thigh.

"We have to go for a drive first." I swing my key ring from my pointer finger and catch the bundle in my palm.

"Don't want to whip it out at the table?" she purrs.

"It's not here," I say giving a shrug and letting her stew in confusion.

Her hand caresses my crotch. My dick jumps to press harder against the fabric.

"Feels like it is to me," she says coyly despite the wicked smirk that ghosts her lips.

"Let's go trouble maker," I say and she slides from the booth.

I allow myself to count to three while staring at the skin of her back, the curve of her hips, and then adjust myself on my way up from the table as discretely as possible.

Pressing a hand to the exposed skin of her back, we make our way out slowly. We're stopped every few feet for me to give cheek kisses or shake hands with another friendly face.

Twenty minutes later, we're in the car slowly driving through the neighborhood. Cool night air breezes by us, a smattering of stars dot the sky. It's the sort of night that feels magical. Even the moon is out again, returning from the darkness of the nights prior. The waxing crescent adds a bit more glow. We turn onto 8th Street, or *Calle Ocho*, and I wait. My heart pounds in my chest, my skin tingles and I want to shout for her to notice the series of large rooster statues. The 'Rooster Alley' has been part of the neighborhood since I was a little boy, and when I turned enough profit to commission one, it was a big deal.

She's lightly touching her face, glancing around as I slow the car to a full stop. I watch intently as her eyes go wide, glowing in the streetlight. Her breath hitches and then she exhales a slow tittering laugh that grows until she's completely breathless.

"Shut. Up. Shut the fuck up," she heaves out between laughs.

"Meet my cock," I try to deadpan, but the laughter is too contagious and sweeps through us, around us. My body is warm, I feel alert like I had five espresso shots and did a line of cocaine. I can't recall the last time I felt this alive after a long dinner service come two AM.

"Does your cock have a name?" she asks, breathy and radiant. There's nothing but pure joy pour out of her, like she's the spirit of Christmas itself, but how can that make sense? Does Christmas magic visit even when you don't celebrate?

I bite my lip, humming thoughtfully. "You can go take a look. You can touch it. You can even take a photo of my cock." I snicker feeling like a teenager for uttering that sentence.

She opens the car door and walks in a steady circle, examining the rooster sculpture from all angles. Finally, she looks over at the car and says, "Your cock is huge. It's pretty too. Nicely decorated."

"His name," I remind her, and point to the little sign on a stake in the ground next to the art. She takes her phone from a tiny bag and uses the flashlight to illuminate the plaque clearly.

"Gallo Pinto was donated by the Hakimi Family Foundation," she reads loud enough for me to hear.

"What was that, Blondie?"

"The Hakimi Family Foundation donated this," she repeats sliding back into the passenger seat.

"Correct." I give a firm nod.

"Cute. Not the cock I expected, and what is Gallo Pinto?" Her face scrunches, the way she's processing this information is written all over her features.

"Well, this is the cock Javi told me to show off, so I brought you to see the rooster statues and Gallo means rooster, and Gallo Pinto is a rice and beans dish from Nicaragua and Costa Rica. It was practically all I ate when I was traveling there," I say, flicking the signal and pulling away from the curb. "Where now?"

"This is your tour, have anything else we must do? Is there a collection of pearl necklaces you want to give me? Maybe you'd like to go to a spit roast together?" She flubs the joke and laughs at herself in irritation. "Ugh, I did not pull that off," she whines.

"I can pull off whatever you need me to, honey," I say and then take her hand and kiss her knuckles. "But, since you skipped the underwear, that would leave you fully exposed."

"You want to go skinny dipping with me?" She perks up.

"That sounds nice, you got a private pool somewhere here we can hit up?" I tease.

She looks out at the bay below us on the MacArthur Causeway and cocks a brow.

"Nope. Not going into the ocean at night. Tomorrow we can go to the nude beach if you still want to swim naked." I place her hand on her thigh and squeeze. "If you really can't wait to get wet, I can always come up with some suggestions."

I can hear her breath hitch and slow as she waits.

"No smart mouth replies?" I ask and she exhales low and even.

I cock a brow, though I'm not sure if she can see it since my eyes are on the road.

"Jury is still out, what would that involve?"

———

TO MY RIGHT, the bombshell that dropped into my lap tonight is asleep on her window. Chin slumped to chest, jaw soft, eyelids relaxed. Her whole face is tranquil.

I hate to disrupt her looking so soft, but we've pulled up to her hotel a few minutes ago and I've delayed for as long as possible.

I start by lightly nudging her left arm. I run a hand over her silky skin. "Wake up sleeping beauty, we're back," I coo softly, testing how responsive she is right now.

She waves a dismissive hand and gives the softest whine in response to being woken up. "Want me to carry you?" I tease while unbuckling her seatbelt. Gently, to ensure it doesn't snap and hit her, I follow it back toward the door to guide it away.

"Maybe you should," she says.

"Can I get you without flashing everyone, panty free party girl?" I tease.

"Oh. Shit." She slides her legs together toward the door and the hotel valet opens it for her. Giving a slight jog, I make my way around the hood and help guide her with one arm around her waist. She's pressed into my side, her sweet scent rising from her hair as she tucks further into me.

The walk through the lobby, to the elevator bank, and then the ride up to her floor are all soft silence. We're in a bubble of our own making, the sleepiness she's cloaked in mixed at the edges with something more electric.

The steel doors open, and we make our way to the door of her hotel room again.

"This is where I leave you, sleepy head. I can text you tomorrow and we can hang out again soon," I offer, knowing she's a zombie. That bone tired that sets in after working hard and trying to live it up during the brief pauses.

"No phone numbers. No socials," she says with a seriousness despite the pout of her lips.

Bending forward I press my mouth to hers, stealing a kiss.

"No contact information at all?" I'm taken aback by the thought.

"Let's just sleep, we'll figure it out after," she offers with a shrug.

Having slept in worse places than a luxury South Beach hotel, I can't complain and watch as she digs out the keycard. The lights blink red, and she tries again holding the card to the reader. On the third attempt, the lights blink green and the gears make the mechanical sound of the lock opening fills the quiet hallway.

Pushing the heavy door in, I let Shae take the lead into her hotel room. I watch as it closes behind us, before flipping the deadbolt and adding the secondary lock. She stumbles a bit as she moves to her bag, pulling out an adorable pair of pajamas and walking into the bathroom.

I grab my toothbrush and boxers and stand outside the small, tiled space watching in awe. Despite her haziness, she takes a bottle and a washcloth and begins to wipe the makeup from her face gently. Turning the knobs, the faucet runs and she gives a few touch-tests and adjustments before lathering up with the soap from a second bottle. Next, she pats her face dry and lines up a series of small bottles and tubes before conducting a multi-step routine that I can officially say would be possible for her to complete in her sleep.

Once she's completed the face care routine, she drops her dress and steps into the shorts. They are bright blue boxers with stripes of rainbow lights printed on them, dangling from a squiggly black line. Before adding her shirt, I can see from the angles of the mirror her naked chest in the reflection. She. Has. Her. Nipples. Pierced. I adjust myself in my jeans.

Damn, I missed those before.

The tank top she pulls on is white, and the metal presses against it leaving the piercing visible. The more I stare, the thicker my cock grows in my pants, the less comfortable jeans are.

I can't stand it anymore and yank the top button of the fly, before pulling to release all five closures. I make quick work of switching my pants for my red boxer briefs and saunter into the bathroom.

There, Shae has the cold water running and is getting ready to brush her teeth. I beat her to placing my bristles under the water and give her a sly smile in the mirror. She nudges me silently, and pushes her brush closer to the top of the tap. We go another two rounds, nudging each other and pressing our brush up higher until I'm unable to top hers.

"Ha!" she cries out in victory, then pulls her brush from the sink and adds toothpaste. She continues to do a victory dance as she brushes. Her ponytail swishes down her back and her hips shake to a song only she can hear.

I'm so wrapped up in her movement, I almost forgot why I was in here with her. When she turns to the sink and spits, I'm shaken from my lust-filled haze and remember that I'm *also* supposed to be brushing my teeth. I grab the tube and squeeze a dot out and begin to brush along watching her continue the victory dance. Her movements are graceful, I wonder if she danced growing up. I wonder if she would tell me the truth if I asked.

I lean in, drinking from the tap to swish the remnants of the toothpaste from my mouth. Emptying the water into the sink noisily, it cuts her from her reverie, and I can't help but smile wider. She's enchanting.

"What's with the get up?" I ask, noticing now that her shirt says Vixen out of the same string light print, and has a leaping reindeer over it.

"I know *technically* I'm not supposed to, but I've always really loved Christmas things. The cookies. The movies. The magic of it all! So, since I'm not home with my ex-Orthodox Mom and very anti-assimilation Dad, I treated myself to some Christmas pajamas for this trip." The wide grin, the light in her tired eyes, gives the aura of someone used to sneaking around.

"Well, thank goodness I packed my red boxers to sleep in. I can be your Santa, *baby*," I say returning her relaxed grin. "But I'm only coming after you get some rest, let's go, Prancer."

"Aw, poor chef can't read. It says *Vixen*," she teases me.

"Yes, but you are flitting around like you are used to prancing through life. I think you got the wrong shirt. Now, giddy up." I give a playful smack to her ass and we turn in for the night.

shae

THE NEXT MORNING, a bright streak of sunlight cuts through the room and hits me directly in the eyes. Stretching my arms overhead, I let out a groan. "Ugh."

Turning to my side I see a tan man. Taller than me, but not the largest guy around. His thick muscular form is stocky. Short but strong. With his stomach pressed into the mattress and his face turned away, it takes a minute to jog my memory until I see the large lion tattoo across his back on display. The stained couch, the apology gift from the caterer, the handsome chef weaving stories. The way he looks dangerous but was tender and, given how he ate pussy, extremely generous.

The lion's face is calm, his mane long and appears wind swept. The bold black lines are mesmerizing and I'm unable to stop myself from tracing them. Using the point of my manicured nail to lightly scratch the figure. He stirs slightly, releasing a soft moan. The deep, guttural sound repeating and drawing me closer to him. Sitting alongside his ribs, I notice a new image. His other side had the Hamsa and pomegranate, because here is a large knotty tree with olives hanging from the branches. I scratch along the design, realizing the roots trail into his boxers and so I continue along the waistband.

"Hey Blondie," he says, voice gravelly with sleep.

"Yeah, Brownie?" I ask and tip my finger barely under the elastic band.

"Are you into edging me?" he asks lower still. He sounds strangled by lust. The tension surrounding us begins to thicken.

I press my lips to his shoulder to smother a laugh, and he heaves a resigned sigh.

"Fuck. Baby. Follow your instincts," he says with a deep moan. It makes his body vibrate beneath me.

I take my tongue to every drawing I hadn't explored yet. The crossed chef's knives, the symbols and words blurring into the feel and taste of him.

Simon's hips roll against the mattress as I explore from his shoulders to his waistband once. Twice. On the third time, I bite at the waistband and pull. Releasing my teeth, the snap of the elastic reverberates sharp and quick.

In response, he writhes again, and another moan escapes his lips.

"You're dry humping the mattress," I chastise with a teasing lilt.

I go to remove his underwear, and he quickly turns over taking a defensive stance. He launches toward me with hands splayed.

A mix of momentum and gravity take over. Next thing I know, he's flipped us so he's hovering above me. His nose finds my neck, and he nuzzles me before tracing collarbone to ear, nipping and kissing along the way. The breathy noises on my exhale betray my growing need.

He kisses toward my mouth, then pauses to pull back. Our eyes meet. I take in the full image of him over me. Studying his arm muscles as they work to hold him, tensed and straining to keep his full weight off me. Lowering my gaze, I can make out a bit of the painfully strained fabric as it struggles to hold his erection.

Desperate for friction I try to roll my hips forward. I need his firm length against my throbbing core. He tries to move away, brushing a hair a bit too gently from my face for my liking. I seize control back as he's lost in thought by hooking my heels over his ass and slamming our bodies together. The relief of the pressure against me is instantaneous, then it's once again not enough.

"Kiss me," I command, and our lips crash into a feverish match. I want him naked. I need to be naked. Now. Ten minutes ago. My body is engulfed in the heat of our embrace.

We wind tongues and lips, our limbs and bodies roll; there's an ongoing war for dominance. Sparks fly around us and between us off sweat slicked skin. With each tumble we take across the king-size mattress, one of us holds the keys. It doesn't seem to matter if I'm pinned or pinning, each moment is more thrilling than the last.

While on top, I shed my tank. I grab his waistband and pull it as I crawl backward toward the end of the bed.

Removing his feet from the boxers, his shorts fall to the floor a moment before mine join them. The way my lungs fight for breath rivals the thumping in my chest. My pussy aches from staring at the way his long, thick shaft stands proud. From this angle, I see his balls pulling tight to his body, all surrounded by well-groomed hair. The soft, dark hair along his calves and thighs matches his forearms and chest.

I study his face for a moment. He's statuesque with the chiseled jaw, strong line of his prominent nose, and large eyes full of wonder.

"Come back," he says. It hits me with a bit of a command and a bit of a whine, like he can't decide what happens next either.

I sink my teeth into my lower lip and shake my head to continue cataloguing every inch of skin and ink on display.

His dick twitches in the air, a glistening pearl of precum rises to the top. Simon nods and motions me forward with his fingers in a gesture that causes me to clench around nothing. His chest rises and falls on a noisy breath. Placing my hands on the mattress, I push forward and end up on all fours.

"Crawl to me Blondie," he grits out and I straddle his legs to make sure he is tortuously close but not touched as I make my way forward.

Faced with his impressive girth, I loosen my jaw and give it a teasing lick. Enough to break the growing anticipation without fully shattering it. I continue forward, leaving a trail of spit mixed with precum along his stomach as I make my way toward kissing him once more.

"Is that all I get after I had you for dessert on my counters?" he asks, brow cocked and mouth smirking.

"Is this supposed to be some sort of reciprocal system?" I say with the intention to counter his reply.

"I'd be very happy to reciprocate while you suck my cock if you turn around, Blondie."

Rocking my hips backward, his erection grazes my slick folds, and I'm lost to the desire to notch him to my entrance then ride him to the finish line or give in to his request.

"Fuck. Blondie. You feel so good," he says and I moan appreciatively in response.

"I'm not going to be able to stop thinking about how you tasted. I need more, Blondie. Sit on my fucking face while you swallow this cock," he cries.

Firm hands grasp my hips and yank me hard until my clit is pressed to his nose. He inhales and moans, like this is a fine wine. Adjusting his position to lick a long line from above my clit, his path follows down sensitive spots and between lips, until he presses his tongue inside me.

"Oh my god," I cry with a moan, as loud as I want because I'll never see any of these people again. I'm going to soak in every moment of pleasure as I ride his tongue and lips. Hands holding me hard enough that I'm confident there will be five tiny fingerprints on me. I'm writhing along with his movements, sighing and moaning.

My pebbled nipples and the barbells reflect the stripe of morning light from the window. Tensed muscles are within seconds of the ecstasy of release when everything stops.

"If you want to come, you'll turn around and swallow me like the naughty girl you are," he says. A crack rings out as his palm strikes my ass.

Fuck. "Do it again," I whine, and he chuckles.

"Not until you—" he starts to repeat.

I cut off the statement, meeting his request, swallowing him to the back of my throat. Pulling back with an audible pop, I pause to pool the saliva in my mouth. Dipping down once more, this time I add warmth and wet him until his body hair tickles my nose.

With each aggressive stroke of his length with my mouth our murmurs and moans grow and echo in the space. I hear a wet pop from behind me and his thumb draws between my lips, mixing my arousal with his spit. The splay of his hand holds firm to the curve of my ass, while his thumb presses against the puckered entrance.

All at once there's pressure and he's pushed into me. His mouth covers my pussy and his thumb works in and out of me, all with equal fervor. I feel his next groan against my cunt as it vibrates to his throaty sounds. His hips thrust forward, continuing to push him deeper still and the sounds of him fucking my mouth fill the air around us. After another rough thrust to the back of my throat, he yanks my clit into his mouth. There's suction and teeth and it brings me to the brink of pain before suddenly there's an explosion of pleasure. My legs are shaking, his cock is throbbing inside my mouth as hot ropes of cum paint the back of my throat.

Pulling away, I fall to the side with a head on his hip my knee knocked against his shoulder.

He rises to his knees and looks at me, a look somehow sated and heated at the same time.

"Let me see you swallow, Blondie." He presses a thumb to my lip, and I obey.

However, before he can utter a word of praise I snap, "That better not be the hand that was just in my asshole."

simon

TWISTING THE BATHROOM DOORKNOB, it swings back. I'm using one of the white fluffy towels to dry my hair then drop it back onto the tile. Strutting forward into the carpeted space, I look around and find Shae setting up a spread of room service.

"All yours," I say. I kiss her temple and grab a grape from a fruit platter to pop in my mouth. She turns away from the rolling cart, the soft terry bathrobe she slipped into tickling my chest.

"You're," she says on a hitched breath.

Yanking the belt open, I slide my hands into the material and over her shoulders. "Uh huh. Now you are too," I say around the food as I chew.

"Get cleaned up, we have something to do before it's too late and I can't show you a spot I guarantee nobody else will take you to," I say swatting her butt.

While Shae showers, I get dressed and polish off two cups of coffee from the carafe. I peek through the cloches and find one with a series of cold options including more fruit, lox, yogurt, and hard-boiled eggs. The second has large, fluffy pancakes. While the final one has a plate of scrambled eggs, bacon, sausage, and a pile of buttered toast. Grabbing one corner, I bite with a satisfying crunch and butter runs over my tastebuds.

"Your food is getting cold," I shout over the noise of the hair dryer.

"Huh?" she calls back.

"The food," I shout.

"Huh?" she repeats, this time lowering the device to a softer whirring.

"The food is getting cold," I say waving a hand over the display. Biting into the toast again, I chew and watch her return to the full blast assault of heat. Shrugging, I plate the eggs and meat onto two triangles of toast with a healthy dash of hot sauce and dig in. Fuck, this is hitting the spot. It's not that it's good so much as it's filling. After everything we did to each other, I'm starving. I could eat army rations and it would be good.

Once I down a second sandwich, I check her progress. At least she's applying makeup now. I hope that means she's almost ready. Checking the time on my watch, I can't believe it's already afternoon. A quick search confirms that the flea market I want to take her to see is open for a few more hours, and we have to cut across town. Stepping behind her in the bathroom, I place my hands softly on her shoulders. Leaning forward, so my breath caresses her skin, I whisper, "What are you going to eat, sweetheart? You can't expect me to finish that all. Do you need coffee? Let me get you a plate while you finish going from stunner to knock out."

A natural flush spreads across her face, and I kiss her neck watching the pink hue grow on her chest. "Come on Blondie, either you tell me what to make you, or I'll have to guess. I like feeding people."

"You like to eat too," she teases.

"I just had hot sauce; you want that on your pussy?" I balk. "I'm not going to do that. Food. Now."

"A yogurt and berries," she says before quickly calling out, "and coffee. Only a tiny splash of cream. Thank you."

I'm building her a parfait and coffee plate when I watch the towel wrapped around her slide down. She pulls on a red bathing suit, or maybe it's one of those clothes-not-swimming-things, and a pair of cut off denim.

"Have this, then I'm taking you on the town before Christmas shuts everything down," I prompt.

———

FORTY-FIVE MINUTES later we're finally in the car to my secret stop, The Flea. Another forty-five minutes on the road and we pull into the lot by the beige stucco building. There are multiple arches showing off the entrances, and a series of food trucks line the curb outside. The giant palm tree trunks are wrapped in colorful large bulb lights. A giant inflatable Santa wearing sunglasses and a flamingo print shirt flutters in the light breeze. As we exit the car, I grab Shae's hand and lead her through the lot to the automatic double doors. Once inside, there's a cacophony of Spanish and English conversation. Whirring blenders from stalls serving juice and smoothies mix with the dulcet tones of each stalls' music selection.

It reminds me of the oldest markets worldwide—Jerusalem, Athens, Rome, and Istanbul all had a mix of food, clothing, luxury items with dubious discounts and tacky shirts. Yet, if you knew the best corners there was also the family who made the same pastry there for the last century. Sure, The Flea is an exercise in wading through watered down perfume and pirated movies, but then there's the gems. The tea and spices are out of this world, and the bulk candy and nuts prices can't be beat. Which, if we're about to spend the next twenty-four hours in bed at her hotel, I'm going to want snacks.

"Is there a good spot for iced coffee?" Shae asks me, pleadingly.

"Drip at the hotel wasn't hitting the spot?" I tease, then guide her toward a stall and wait in line quietly together. She seems dazed, but I'm unsure with the large sunglasses obscuring her eyes.

"Dos cafécito helados, por favor," I say placing an order.

"What did you get?" she asks, rocking from side to side and pulling my arm along with her.

"Two Cuban iced coffees. They're made from dark roast espresso brewed in a stovetop espresso maker then stirred with a luscious sugar foam. These are cooled to serve over ice and a bit of condensed milk is added. They're strong, sweet, and can really wake you up," I explain while passing her the to-go cup.

Her lips part, taking a deep inhale, she lets out a soft moan. "Oh baby," she whispers reverently after a sip. "Thank you, sweet baby Jesus in the manger."

"Okay, Ricky Bobby, slow down. This is meant to be savored," I say, slinging my arm over her shoulders.

"Does that make you the one he's in step-brothers with?" she asks, lifting her sunglasses to examine me.

We laugh and compare favorite movies, music, and books as I lead the way to my favorite spot. There's multiple stalls for bulk candy and nuts, but one in particular always cuts me a deal and throws in a few extra items to try. I collect a full canvas tote of small bags filled with dried fruit, sweet gummy candy, sour candy, and seasoned mixes of pistachios, cashews, and peanuts. I'm pumped to hit up the trucks out front, but Shae pauses long enough to yank me back a step.

"Hey, Si," she says eyeing a thrifted clothing store.

"Hey, Shae," I say mimicking her tone.

"I have an idea," she says. Her mouth twitches into a sly smile, her eyes light up, and her energy is palpable.

"Maybe I shouldn't have given you a Cafecito," I say, part teasing but a little worried.

"You can dress me however you want," she offers starting to

make her way toward Wynwood Wore What? looking back with the most come hither stare I've seen in real life.

"Here's how it's going to work. Give me your phone," she says.

"I thought you didn't want my number?" I poke because I've never known when to leave well enough alone.

"Open your timer, set it up for twenty minutes. When I say go, we both press start. When the timer goes off, meet me over there," she says and points out a dressing room with a floor to ceiling curtain.

"Ready?" I ask, cocking a brow.

"Ready," she says, eyes narrowed and competitiveness oozing from her every pore.

"Set?" I continue the standard phrase.

"Go!" she shouts and takes off toward the men's section.

In a stupor, I stand and watch for a bit as she pushes the hangers quickly and raises up item after item to examine.

"Chop chop, chef!" she calls out across the store where my feet have seemingly nailed themselves to the floor boards.

"Shit," I grit out and turn toward the women's section now unclear if we're going for cute, for funny, for sexy.

The row closest to me holds a number of silk babydoll dresses that look too intimate to be okay to wear second hand. I move to the next rounded clothing rack and choke back a laugh as I pick up increasingly hideous dresses. The tag reads house coat/mumu and I hold onto one that has an animal print. The next rack has a series of track suits from the late 80s and early 90s in a series of neon patterns. I come across a coral and teal knock off football windbreaker and grab that too.

Despite being a fashion forward man, I'm facing the wall of denim as a thirty-three-year-old. Shit. Okay, she looks young, but I don't know. We didn't discuss ages. Does she realize I'm in my thirties? How old does she think I am?

Except then it hits me, the snow washed 80s denim. They're a high contrast pair, light with dark specks. No matter what those tapered waists never came back in style. With the jacket I'm on a roll to make it themed, only I need a few more items.

I look at my alarm. Five minutes to go, I jog to the table of T-shirts and grab the bin labeled for music. Digging around, I find the perfect black and neon tee from none other than Debbie Harry's Blondie.

I hear my alarm blaring mixed with hers across the room. Head swiveling around the store, my eyes finally land on her near the oversized armchair and a three-way mirror. There are two hideous mustard yellow-brown curtains draped in front of changing rooms, pulled to the side and settled into tarnished gold hooks. They don't match, each one ornate in its own way. One looks like two twisted strands ending in an oversized leaf, while the other has some sort of minimalist design with clean lines and sharp edges.

"What did you bring me?" Shae asks, eyes wide with delight. Her impatient grabbing gestures are so adorable but make me want to delay her further.

"You first, this was your idea," I say.

"At the same time?" she counter offers.

Stepping back into the leaf fitting room, I follow her and gaze upon the most hilarious mix of blazers, pants, and vests from different three-piece suits. Touching each piece the mix of fabrics and colors make it hard to not want to laugh at the plaid polyester vest to the brown corduroy sport coat with large, wide notch lapels. Then there's the pants, grape purple flared suit pants.

"Did you raid Ron Burgundy's closet?" I teasingly ask.

"Who?" The way her eyebrows quickly go up her hairline and furrow are so adorable.

"Ron Burgundy, the Anchorman, the Will Farrell movie..." I slowly trail off.

"I've heard of it, yeah, it's from the 1970s. What did you get me?" she says, trying to peer at the pile in my arms.

"I went a decade later for you, Blondie," I say waving the T-shirt for her to see.

"Cute. What else?" She bites her lip and damn do I want to do that again.

I hand her the jeans and windbreaker and wait for a reaction.

"Oh my god, I love it. All of it. Perfect. Let's try them on." She squeals brightly while pulling the curtain closed.

The magnetic pull to her takes over. I press her against the wall and smash our mouths together, stealing any momentary confusion. Her kiss back is softer than our morning sex. This is more languid and paced. Her lips and tongue take their time exploring mine. Her hands move to the button of my shorts, and I feel the fabric slide to my feet. Copying her move, I undo her shorts and press them over her hips.

At that moment, a deep throaty cough interrupts us. "Excuse me, hi, I'm just letting you know our policy is one person per fitting room unless it's a disability accommodation."

"Thank you, I'm just helping him to try on his outfit," she says muffling her laugh into my chest.

"Ok, but, because of theft, we do have security cameras in the general area. We don't generally review the footage, but you know... so you are aware," the voice says before the sound of retreating footsteps.

A giggle continues to pepper my chest with the heat of her breath, her skin, and I can't help but fall apart too.

shae

"I NEED PHOTOS FOR MY FAMILY," I say while holding out my phone to Simon. Strutting over to the three-way mirror to adjust the oversized tee. I tuck the hem into the band of my bra to fake a crop top. Now that it billows over the high waisted denim to show off the pleats, I take the windbreaker over one shoulder and strike a pose. He takes a few from different angles, and his keen eye for presentation shows as I flip through the images.

"Don't I get to be in one?" Simon asks, jutting his lower lip out in an exaggerated pout.

I place a fist below my chin, stone faced in my thinking pose. Moving my hands to create a box, I look mimicking a director examining a shot.

"Aw, Blondie, come on. You know you'll wanna show me off when you get back to..." he trails off.

"Philly," I answer quickly. Shit. I shared something. Why am I telling him stuff he doesn't need to know? Except, I kind of want him to know. "Has this always been home?"

"For a while now, yeah. Came here after culinary school. Worked in a number of different resort kitchens, with my Uncle

Eli's catering company, and finally opened Sin this past fall. Just in time for the snow birds," he says, chest jutting forward as pride washes over his face.

"Stop trying to distract me. Come closer." He pulls us together to take a few quick photos of us with my phone before handing it back. "If I can't have your number, can you air drop them?"

"Maybe," I say, extending the sound.

"Is that Stevie Nicks?" I hear a deep, jolly voice call from across the room. His following belly laugh is a spot on impression of Santa's and when I catch the speaker, they are even donning the notorious red and white stocking cap.

"Saul, hi. Fancy to see you again," I say brightly, absorbing some of his sunny demeanor. Turning to wave a hand between the two men, I make introductions. "Simon. Saul. We met on the flight down. First he says pine is his favorite scent, now the hat. I'm starting to question if he's *actually* Santa." My face hurts from how big my smile is.

"Hi, Simon Hakimi." Simon puts out a hand to shake but Saul uses it to pull Simon forward with an *oomph* and hug him.

"You, young man, are going big places," Saul says giving a loud clap on the back at the end of his embrace.

"Me?" Simon asks, quirking a brow and glancing at me with confusion.

"What are you doing out on Christmas Eve dressed like my best years anyhow?" Saul turns to ask me.

"We're trying to find things that are open to do over Christmas," I answer, hoping Saul will have suggestions.

"Hmm. How do you feel about a little Borsch Belt comedy?" he says.

Simon and I exchange a lingering glance. There's a strange telepathic thing happening between us. We're both grinning, clearly enticed by whimsy and adventure. There's no way I will turn down a Lenny Bruce impersonator or whatever it is.

"Tell you what, if you come with me in these outfits, I'll pay for them. But you, young lady—" Saul says cutting himself off sharply mid-sentence. He waves a finger to signal one moment, then returns with large gold coins in his palm.

"Hanukkah gelt?" I ask, too far to see the detailing.

"No, ho, ho, ho. These are the type of earrings that all the gals wore back then. It completes the look," he says giving another belly laugh.

Saul waves to the store clerk. "Hey Rita, I'm going to cover their tab. Can I pull the tickets and bring them up?"

While Saul and Rita settle the bill I fold our clothes into a neat pile. Simon comes around me, his arms close as he picks up his own items. Soft enough for only me to hear, he whispers, "If you don't want to do this say the word. We can make up an excuse. But, I kind of want to see if they have someone pretending to be Lenny Bruce."

"Shut up. That's what I was thinking. Also, if this Catskills style show is anything like *Dirty Dancing* I expect you to do the Swayze lift for me," I say.

"Do you want to carry the watermelon?" he asks. When our eyes meet in the mirror he gives a hearty wink, his mouth open in a toothy grin. In the harsh fluorescent lighting, I notice that his eyes wrinkle deeply with the smile and a few strands of silver are mixed in around the temples.

Interesting. Okay *zaddy*. My pulse drops low in my belly and my muscles clench. Do I have a thing for older men now?

I work on packing our clothes into the tote bag Simon leaves with me while he heads back to the register. When I join the two men at the counter, Saul is handing Simon back his phone with the maps app open.

"Follow me to the lot, I'll point out my car and then you can follow me to that address."

"Sounds good, thanks." Simon says.

CROSSING the lot and sliding into the soft leather seats, we exhale and our eyes meet. A laugh escapes me, and he joins in, giddiness filling the space between us. It feels like there's sparks of glitter swirling around.

My delight is cut short when I notice the way his dark brow is furrowed, the pucker of his cheek where his teeth have sunk into the scruffy flesh. He gives a deep inhale. I count. Two. Three. Four.

"You wavering?" I gently ask, reaching my hand to his over the gear shift.

"It's almost an hour away. In Boca," he says the word Boca with puckered lips, like he bit a lemon.

"Not a fan of Boca?" I ask despite seeing it all over his face.

Simon hesitates, darting out his tongue to part his lips and lick them. He swallows thickly, then relaxes into a shy smile. Pushing the air from his lungs out his mouth, his cheeks puff like a blowfish and I giggle. "Nah. I'm good," he says.

"You look like that fish that puffs up… a blowfish. You scared, Si?" I try to say sincerely, but the giggles continue to break through.

Grumbling in what I can only describe as his *kitchen voice*, he scoffs. "I don't like driving with the grandparents. They're unpredictable. After dark is worse. But, whatever." He shrugs and puts the car in gear to back out of the spot.

"Oh. Mood. I got this," I say while pulling up the perfect playlist.

As Frank Sinatra, Dean Martin, and Billie Holiday croon about magical, wonderful, moments this time each year we tail Saul. A beautiful rendition of "Santa Clause is Coming to Town" is abruptly cut off when my phone rings. I silence it so the song can continue without checking the caller ID. A moment later, it rings again and I momentarily panic that I sent my boss to voicemail. *Shit.*

Exhaling when, *nope*, it's my family. The missed calls are paired with texts on texts in the sibling chat asking who is behind me in the mirror taking the photo.

The third time the song is interrupted by my phone ringing, it's no longer my siblings but Mateo calling. Damnit. Swiping, I pick up his video call.

"Hi," I say on an extended whine slipping into little sister mode.

"Yes. Still the favorite. 'Sup," he says giving a quick chin lift.

"On my way to a comedy show, you?" I answer hoping to distract him enough and end the call.

"Cool. Cool. Cool. On Christmas Eve?" he asks. His brow furrows and relaxes, and I can picture my sister behind the phone camera mouthing *Jewish* to him.

"Yeah, honestly, I think it's going to be full of a bunch of grandparents," I say, hoping that is enough detail.

His eyes look off camera for a moment and he says, "Yeah, that tracks. That's dope. You don't strike me as the type to hang with the oldies often. Anyway, we wanted to check in because we miss you party girl." Like always, my sister's golden retriever puppy of a boyfriend is so affable and easy-going I forget that she's right there.

"Aw, buddy. It's okay. I'm enjoying myself," I say, shaking off the slight homesickness that bounces around my chest and squeezes my heart.

"Not too much, I hope," I hear my sister call out and automatically everything I might have been homesick for evaporates. In the tiny video screen I watch my eyes roll so ferociously, I'm surprised I couldn't see my brain.

"Gorgeous," Mateo says softly, his eyes off screen on my sister.

"Hey! You called him a bad idea for months before you admitted to what was going on between you two, can you climb down off that pedestal now, please?" I call as if they are far from the phone.

They may as well be, she's come back to his side and he's wrapped one long arm around her. They are all scrunched noses and longing gazes.

"Gross, can you not do this foreplay thing right in front of me?" I squeal. I blow a raspberry in disgust.

"Whoa, you're in a Lambo aren't you?" Mateo says, jumpy with a sudden epiphany.

"Umm," I stammer, my eyes flit to Simon.

"She is," Simon says loudly.

"Oh, you're with a boy," they tease like they weren't asking who he was over text.

"Yep. Now I'm being super rude so, gotta go, bye!" I rush out and hang up.

"Take it you have a big family?" Simon asks, eyes on the road, one hand on the steering wheel, the other holding my thigh.

"Something like that," I grumble.

He lightly strokes his thumb along the mottled fabric causing my tense muscles to soften.

"I have a huge extended family back in Los Angeles," Simon offers and I give a non-committal *uh huh* in reply.

My thoughts are like the bouncy balls from a quarter vending machine. An avalanche of them have broken loose and are frolicking aimlessly through the corridors of my mind. This feels really nice, like we aren't practically strangers. I bet he'd get along great with Mateo. I'm not here to get to know him.

Rein it in, girl. This is just an adventure. This is a story so that someday, when I look back on my own life I don't want to puke.

"My Uncle Eli, the caterer you're working with, is one of my dad's six siblings. He's the oldest, Uncle Eli, so I didn't know him super well growing up. He was already out here."

I let his family story wash over me as the drive continues. Stewing, I rapidly fire off a text.

. . .

FAM JAM [NESSA, Mateo, Shae, Tal, Joshua, Mom-ICE, Dad]
Shae: I'm F I N E. I'm here for W O R K. I'm not a baby, and I don't need you calling and texting me for the next twenty-four hours. I'm taking this vacation day off fully.
Mom-ICE: What's wrong, Shae'Na Maidela?

THE BIT of homesickness pops up for a moment as my mom calls me the Yiddish for *pretty girl* right away. I sigh, knowing I've fully gotten lost in my thoughts when Simon's monologue pauses.

"I didn't think my story was that bad." It's a soft tease, a gesture to move on.

"Sorry, yes, I have a big family. I'm the second of four, and my perfect older sister has the best boyfriend ever and sometimes I forget that because I enjoy his company, I'm actually feeding her information. Now I'm dealing with how to reply to my mom." I bite out the word perfect and know I sound like a petulant child but that's what dealing with her does to me. I could scream and stomp a foot.

I want to be friends. *Someday.* I also don't want to think about this.

"I don't mean to be a buzzkill, but, my job and family are stressful. I don't often get a lot of time to myself. I just wanted a fucking break," I admit, gaze on the way his thumb continues to stroke my thigh. He gives a tight squeeze.

"Okay. We'll take a *fucking* break. Emphasis on *fucking*. I can't wait to get my cock back inside you," Simon says with a devilish grin his voice lowering to a gravely masculine tone.

"Will this be the cock in your pants, or are you hoping to see if I can somehow handle that statue?" I deadpan, holding for the building sexual tension. It cracks and so do we, erupting into laughter together.

78

I drop my phone into my lap. *Screw it, I'll deal with them after Christmas.* Looking up, we've reached the gates of a golf course complex. Saul is chatting with the gate operator and then they wave us through the visitor side into the luxury community for retirees.

shae

SAUL GUIDES us to the large modern clubhouse entry area made of glass panels and steel framing. The recess track lighting and white high ceiling create a bright and inviting environment. The large reflective white tiles have a long, thin carpet of stiff material bisecting the hall. The runner infuses color into the sterile space with its giant monstera leaves in pink and teal.

Reaching the end of the hallway is more of the same vibe, like a hospital curated a jungle. There's a faint scent of cleaner mixed with arthritis cream, and there's no denying this is where you'd find a gaggle of yentas gossiping and discussing the latest accomplishments of their children and grandchildren.

A group of silver haired ladies are whispering and staring at the arrival of our trio. I lean over to Saul and ask, "What's with the Golden Girls?"

"Oh, you mean the Sharons?" His reply is chuffed; this man is always so jovial.

"The Sharons?" Simon repeats.

"Sharon Stein, Gold, Bloom, and Katz, this is my friend Shae. She's an up and comer in public relations I met on the flight home. I just ran into her and this handsome gentleman at The Flea and invited them to join us for tonight's show."

"Oh, that's so sweet of you, Solly," Sharon Gold says with a smile that doesn't quite reach her eyes.

Sharon Bloom tenses and wraps her oversized cardigan closer, crossing her arms. I notice the way they size up Simon and his tattoos suspiciously. I'm growing hot with secondary embarrassment and try to picture slapping the smug look off her face. I mimic Bloom's stance, crossing my arms. Hardening my eyes. It's exhausting to watch her.

"Yes, and this is Simon. He's been gracious enough to spend the day with me since we're both seriously lacking in Christmas plans. Plus, nothing is ever open. It's never fun to be the odd man out on a holiday. Even if it isn't *your* holiday," I begin and watch them all nod in agreement.

Gold purses her lips, and contemplates her words for a moment. Unfortunately, if she'd taken one moment longer it might have been better since she adds an accent I didn't use.

"See-mon, doesn't your family have plans?" Gold asks, and her faux politeness raises my hackles.

I cut off any opportunity for him to reply, cutting in with, "Well, given that this is local celebrity chef, Simon Hakimi." I pause for dramatic effect hoping to embarrass her properly.

"Eli Hakimi's nephew?" I hear Stein whisper to Katz as she adjusts her glasses and makes a show of examining Simon.

"Yes." Simon says.

Simultaneously, I answer, "You may know him from his Michelin star restaurant that opened recently, Sin." There's no smile. I want them to burn with shame. "However, if he wasn't what would prevent Saul from having us visit? Is it the tattoos that have you so verklempt?" I pepper in the Yiddish for emotional while pulling my spine tighter in an attempt to feel taller. This is what talking to my sister does, it makes my thoughts jumble and I assume people are looking down on me—and by

81

extension Simon being with me. The more defensive questions roll around my mind, the angrier I get. The hotter my face feels.

Saul places a hand on my back. "You look warm dear. I'll show you where the beverages are." He gently steers me away.

After we've crossed the room he says, "Okay warrior woman. You need to know *when* to brandish that weapon of yours, even if it's to defend someone worthy." He hands me a small paper cup with water, and I finish it in one gulp.

"Weapon?" I ask feeling my eyebrows move in confusion as my lips twitch to avoid a smile. My moments of righteous anger are usually met with a scolding, not someone seeing me within them. I take a long swallow and empty the cup.

"Weapon. Words are your power. Use them wisely. You scolded four women who, yes, deserved it, but they also could have connections you need. Everything you do represents the brand you're building, so never burn a bridge until you are certain you don't need to cross it," Saul says with a smile and a wink.

"They were being terrible; they were profiling Simon. It was rude and kinda racist," I grumble, crushing the cup in my palm. "No, it was racist."

"You're *right*... just not with *how* you jumped in. That man is skilled not only as a chef, he's worked his way to where he is. Do you think he can't handle a few haters?" Saul asks me, giving a very fatherly look that says we both know the answer here.

I let out a sigh and roll my shoulders back. Tossing the crushed cup into the blue recycling bin and reply with an elongated, "Fine."

"Good. Let's head back."

The doors to the multipurpose room have opened and the Sharons have moved on. Simon is standing by the snacks table, examining the store-bought assorted fruit tray.

"What did the melon do to deserve such scrutiny?" I ask, sliding an arm around his waist and pulling us close.

"There's always too much cantaloupe. I don't get why. It's

always too much cantaloupe," he says, lips pulled tight, eyes continuing to glare down at the orange melon like it's personally offensive.

"Isn't it because it's cost efficient?" I think out loud, giving his mid-section a light tickle in hopes he'll soften. He instantly melts for me.

"Probably," he says with a shrug.

The lights flicker and someone steps up to the microphone on stage. In a heavy New York accent, she asks the room to "Please stahp tawlking and find ya seats."

She introduces the comedian, whose name I immediately forget. He's a short, stogy man in his mid-fifties with thick gray hair and a shiny Rolex.

He opens with a question for the room. "How many Jewish mothers does it take to change a light bulb?" Then drops the punchline at the perfect timing with the voice effect and body language changes to match. His aggrieved sigh and dismissive posture the picture perfect staging to his passive-aggressive answer, "Don't bother. I'll sit in the dark. I don't want to be a nuisance to anybody."

A completely trite punchline, but the delivery and accent cause me to laugh. In fact, for the following fifteen minute set, I let myself linger in the nostalgic aura bouncing between residents. This man brought Boca Raton to the old Catskills resorts of their childhood, and sure the jokes were dated but the euphoria in the room was contagious. As the man closes his set, he announces, "I'll be here all night. Don't forget to tip the waiters. And try the veal."

Simon and I exchange a look and then look to Saul.

"It's barely five," I say, trying to speak softly without going unheard.

"So it *is* dinner time, then." Saul gives us a wink.

I lean to my other side. "We're apparently having the early bird special," I tell Simon as I used my elbow to nudge him in the ribs.

"Sounds like a good story. The time you met Santa on

Christmas Eve and had dinner and an old school comedy show with the retirees," he replies. Catching my elbow with his arm, Si places my forearm along his thigh and begins to draw invisible designs with his pointer finger.

The staff comes around with small glass salad plates made to look like etched leaves. Only, when I take mine it is not heavy enough to be glass. I tap my nails on it realizing that it's plastic; of course it is.

The bed of lettuce is topped with a sopping spoonful of a mayonnaise filled salad choices: egg, tuna, or shrimp. Saul turns to the man with the tray. "No chicken Waldorff tonight?"

The waiter taps his nose and in return Saul takes my plate and returns it to the tray. "Three please, boss."

While we wait for our special salads, a younger comedian steps up. She's beautiful, and dressed in a period costume from the 1960s. Taking the microphone from the stand, she turns to the crowd and says, "Bubbe, thank you for the dress. However, did I *have* to also wear the girdle?"

One of the women laughs and a friend of *Bubbe* shouts to the performer, "It's more authentic. Will help you get in character."

With an uptick in her pacing, the woman turns back to the rest of the audience and gives a soft *pahh* sound. "Can you believe what I put up with at home? It's bad enough that I have to do the cooking and the cleaning. Well, not me. My husband pays someone to come in and do the cleaning twice a week. But the cooking! The cooking!" she laments. She reminds me of a show we watched with my parents a few years ago.

The waiter returns and drops three of the tiny salad plates with us that have the neutral-colored mayo-and-chicken salad mixed with cut up grapes, apples, raisins, and walnuts.

"Sheppie broke a tooth on this a few weeks ago, and now we have to special order it because his lawyer daughter is a real ball buster. It was the only way to keep her from suing the place for the cost of his dental work," Saul says in explanation then turns back to the show.

Meanwhile, the actress continues to complete her set in character, and the more she speaks the more familiar she seems. It was only when she wraps up with the line from the show, that my jaw drops.

"Saul, is that?" I ask, knowing I must look like a fish with my wide eyes and slack jaw.

He simply nods, and laughs. "It's a good thing you're both dressed for another era. You should introduce yourself, she is unhappy with her current rep."

I turn to Simon, who has, while the lights were low moved his jacket to his chair. The top buttons of his shirt are undone low showing off his dark chest hair and the sparkle of his gold chain.

"Go, go. I'm good," he says with a reassuring smile. His eyes crinkle around the sides.

As I prepare to introduce myself to Rachel Borstein, I hear Simon and Saul fall into a conversation about the way Sin's marketing is going. I'm torn between my curiosity and the line I drew between us. It's not my business, but meeting Rachel could be big.

Standing up, I give a quick squeeze to Saul. "This might be the first time Santa gave me something on Christmas. Thank you."

Scurrying over to introduce myself, I'm pleasantly surprised by how easygoing she is about my approach.

"Did your grandma convince you that it was decades comedy night, too?" Rachel giggles looking over my attire.

She's even more stunning up close, and I'm utterly charmed by her greeting. "Worse, this was my idea and then Santa Saul ambushed us at the market and so here we are eating in thrifted clothes unexpectedly. Oh, I see you also got the memo on the secret salad menu," I say pointing toward her plate.

I pause momentarily. Someone of her status may not get approached daily, but in this specific outfit she's utterly recognizable. "I don't want to disrupt your time with your grandma, but Saul mentioned that you've had some issues with your public relations team recently. I'm Shae, currently with Shine PR. I'm considering striking out of my own someday, too."

I bite a nail, hesitating, what do I need to pitch here? The decision is instant; I pitch the dream.

"You are hilarious. Everything that you've been doing off set has been getting a mix of the press deserved," I begin, and a resounding agreement breaks out noisily from the women surrounding her. "It sounds like your grandmother and her friends would agree. I think you deserve better. A beautiful, hardworking, actress like yourself? Someone who is committed to so many social good projects needs representation who believes in her. I'd love to share my ideas with you, if the rumor Saul started that you're seeking new representation is true. Of course, if he is pranking us both then I'd love to give your grandma a few laxatives to slip into his drink tomorrow."

The ladies laugh heartily, and I take a deep breath.

Rachel asks, "Do you have a business card?"

While one of her grandmother's friends say, "That might not be a bad prank, except when you're old it gets harder to *go* so he might appreciate the outcome."

"Judy," one of the other women chastises, while the table laughs.

I've dug a card out and circled my cell phone and added my personal email.

"If you want to avoid Emily's commission, message me here," I say pointing to the add on. "However, if you want her oversight in any work we do together, I completely understand. You'll want to use the other address for that."

Affecting the accent from her character, she lays a hand on the card with dainty precision and says, "You're a doll, Shae. I'll have my assistant reach out to you after the holiday."

Mimicking her cadence, I say, "No you are. I look forward to hearing from you."

I turn to walk back to the men, and pause after a few steps calling out over my shoulder. "Oh! If you had any interest in the New Years party we're behind at The Devotional, I'll add you to the list."

I don't catch her reply, but I make a note to add her anyway. Just in case.

simon

LEAVING Boca on Christmas Eve in the early evening was a snap thankfully. With the car back in hotel parking, I look around at the starry sky and can hear the sound of the ocean a block away from us.

Shae looks at me, large puppy dog eyes and lip pouty, she's practically begging now.

"No night swimming," I say, sternly, shaking my head.

Nodding, she continues to give off begging vibes and relents. "Fine, but walking on the beach is allowed, right?"

Leaning in I capture the pout in a kiss. "You look so pretty when you beg, Blondie. I should put you on your knees and see if it gets better." Skimming along her arm, I take her hand and thread it with mine.

"Who knows, maybe you'll get lucky?" she says, her eyes going cloudy and her movements sultry.

"Do you really want to spend the rest of tonight dressed like this?" I say, waving a hand over our outfits.

My suit is corduroy and polyester. If I don't take it off soon, I'll become a giant puddle. The air isn't *as* humid as the summer, but it's *never* a good idea to be dressed like this. In *Florida*. Nope.

Pulling the clingy shirt away from my chest to air out, I can't deal anymore.

"Scratch that, I'm going to change. You can do whatever you want. I can't go to the beach until I break free from whatever horrible choices they made in the seventies. It's too clingy, I'm going to melt."

I turn and start to slowly head inside, checking my periphery finding Shae following slightly behind. Her movements slower than before, a faraway look on her face.

"I bet they didn't notice back then," she says.

"What? How? It was still hot as balls in the summer," I say.

Placing a hand low on her back, I lightly guide her and try to pick up her pace. When we finally arrive at the elevator bank, I see her continuing to poke her tongue against her cheek.

I push the call button, watching her face betray the gears turning in her head.

The steel doors open, and I push us forward once more. Inside the elevator, and still fanning the sweat from my chest, I undo another button. Then one more.

Our eyes meet along the mirrored wall, and finally Shae's thought solidifies enough to tumble out.

"They were just *so* coked out at the discos. Men in full suits. Drinking. Dancing. You add cocaine to the mix… there was a lot of sweating." She wrinkles her nose in disgust, then shrugs. "Makes sense. Yeah?"

It's in this moment that how little we know about each other starts to come together more clearly. I'm not sure what the right answer will be or what she wants from me so I let her words hang.

"Fine. I think it makes sense," she says and crosses her arms over her chest, chin jutted high.

"I didn't say it didn't make sense, Blondie." With that, the elevator dings and the doors open, and a smile splits her face. "Come on." I wrap an arm around her shoulders and steer us to the door.

89

The moment the door closes behind me, I drop the canvas bag of snacks on the rug and strip down to my boxers. My chest rises as I heave a sigh of relief feeling the cold air conditioning cool my skin.

I leap and fall onto the mattress. The duvet billows around me and I let out a second exaggerated sigh. "Come on, babe. How 'bout a power nap? This is cozy." I pat the bed next to me, and a large yawn escapes. "Just like"—a second yawn sneaks in—"a few minutes?"

Shedding the jeans and coat, Shae stands before me wearing the oversized Blondie tee. Climbing in, she tucks her head on my chest. I pull her close and kiss the crown of her head.

This is nice. It feels sort of. Right. I know I'm not supposed to think that. This girl isn't going to stay. Hell, I don't even know her full name. This is insanity.

Turning on her side, Shae snuggles further into my body. Her soft pink manicured nails scratch along the planes of my stomach sleepily and I find myself twirling her hair mindlessly through my fingers. Laying this way, we both drift off.

———

SOUNDS of a pop song mix with the light swish of the sink come from the other side of the thin bathroom wall. Rolling to my side, I realize the door is wide open, and I'm greeted by the most amazing sight; Shae dancing and primping. Her body is pressed against the sink, her ass rounded by the fold of her body while lithe tan limbs and long hair move in time to the music.

Sensation trills up and down my spine. The warmth flooding my body is overwhelming until I've mindlessly fisted my cock under my boxers. Why am I bothering to fight the fabric? I free myself and kick them to the floor. Stretching my arm overhead, I relax the back of my head against one palm, while the other moves along my shaft in heavy fisted tugs. A low moan slips from my lips and the *mmm* noise causes Shae to drop something on the counter with a plink.

She turns and I know what she's seeing; my eyes locked on her ass, cock thick and swollen. I'm aching to be deep inside her, aching to release the building tension.

"Oh, you're up. You're, like, really up," she says breathlessly.

"Can you blame a man?" I ask, unable to stop my knowing grin or my moan.

She stands tall and turns, with her face me, her tiny tits with their silver decorations on display.

The urgency to touch her is overwhelming and I sit up with my cock still in hand, I let my gaze turn cold. "Hands back on the sink, pretty baby."

I stand and close the distance between us in a few long, quick strides. Shae turns, placing her hands on the sink and her ass in the air for me allowing me to firmly grab her hip and tug her cheeks against my hard length. She lets out an appreciative gasp.

"You like that, don't you? When I call you pretty names but take what I want?"

Our eyes meet in the mirror and I watch as her lips part around a soft exhale. Squeezing my hand tighter on the soft flesh of her hips I confirm, "I'm going to be demanding."

"Yes, please," she continues, breathily, her reply coming out in quick short succession.

"Hard. Fast. I'm about to fuck you like there's no tomorrow," I bark, pushing away any reminders about *tomorrow*.

Instead, I look around the counter at the series of toiletry bags and ask, "Do you have condoms there?"

I trail a hand up her spine lightly watching the goose bumps explode along her flesh.

The heat of her pussy teases my throbbing cock. Caressing her prone body, I reach underneath her to rub the pebbled peaks of her nipples. My hands so large over the palm sized mound, I can massage her surrounding flesh. I pinch one nipple, then massage her full tit to soothe. Rough and gentle touch alternating until my control slips.

Shae reaches forward, God I hope for one of those condoms, we've been reckless despite her saying they're her preference. The toiletry bag turns sideways and a slew of items spill across the middle of the counter: foil packets, a tweezer, lube, and a little velvet bag.

She turns to make quick work of sheathing me then turns, hands back on the sink.

"That's my good fucking girl," I say, landing a swat on her ass.

"What's in here," I ask pulling the velvet bag closer and watching a small plastic dreidel roll our way. As I loosen the strings of the smaller bag and find a bright blue gem peeking from the top.

The sound echoes as Shae's hand claps over the spinning top. It doesn't tumble to the floor, and she lets out a throaty laugh. "Wow, it's your lucky night." She nods at the letter shin facing us, which is usually a loss in the game. It's alternate meaning is *put one in*, and when our eyes meet hers burn with desire.

"You want me to put one in?" I tease, one hand on the silicone plug with a jeweled base and the other on my cock.

"More than one?" she asks with a lifted brow sliding the bottle of lube my way.

I'm never going to be able to look at this game the same, because holy fucking shit balls. "Filthiest game of dreidel I've ever won," I stammer as I pour lube on my hand. She's leaned forward, hips shaking to the music still playing, offering me all of her body.

Using two fingers I swipe from the top of her clit back through her own wetness pooling between her legs and then coat her other entrance. I give every inch of her sensitive spots lingering attention making sure she's truly as excited as I am. Pulling my hand back, I make sure to thoroughly coat the tip of the plug. With one hand on her hip, I slowly press the plug inside to the sound of her soft moans.

With a thundering surge of my hips, I enter her dripping core and can feel the way her muscles are clenched tight. There's nothing soft or playful, this isn't love making. No. It's heated, sweaty, animalistic fucking. I pound into her over and over. I've lost myself to the rhythm of my thrusts.

Shae's panting gives way to shrieks of pleasure. She calls out, "Yes." Encourages me with cries of "Harder" and "More."

Our gazes lock. She whimpers, "I'm so full," as her eyes grow heavy.

Brushing her hair over a shoulder a bead of sweat catches my attention. I crave to extend this experience and follow its path down her neck, between her shoulders, along her spine. It finds another small bead and combines into something bigger and more formidable.

Thrusting deeper still I feel her muscles to tense around me so firm that pleasure races along my spine. Her cunt continues to choke the orgasm from my cock, as her cries increase.

"I'm going to—" I grunt out.

At the same time, she screams, "I'm coming."

Those two words are all it takes for everything to reach the final crescendo. My orgasm is hot, thick, and fast. Pulling back, I watch as thick ropes of cum fill the condom.

I give a hearty thwack against her cheek, the cracking noise that reverberates on the tiled walls. "Wait there," I command and she drops her head and pants over the sink basin.

I discard the condom into the trash. Turning the knobs on the shower, I test the water temperature. When I know it's the right temperature, I slide my arm across her stomach and pull her sideways pressing the front of our bodies together. Dropping a sweet kiss to her lips, I add more kisses all over her face before pressing one to her ear. "Let me clean up my girl," I say.

Leading her under the stream, I kneel before her in the

warmth of the steamy air. Kissing along her hips and down the crease of her thigh, I peer up at her from my knees.

"How many more do you think you have in you right now, pretty baby?" I ask.

She swallows thickly. I plunge two fingers into her cunt, and she releases the sweetest moan. Curling my fingers inside her, I lick the outside of her clit hoping to reach every pleasure point at once.

"Heaven. You taste like heaven," I say reverently.

Her sighs increase, her muscles contract. Using my tongue and teeth to suck, pull, and lave against her throbbing clit I draw out more moans.

"How many?" I ask again between kisses and bites.

"I. I. I. I don't—" I pump my fingers harder as she stammers and then I feel her muscles clamping hard. Her cries increase.

"At least one, because," she pants, "I'm coming." The waves of her release come hard and fast. Her thighs shake, and I grip tight to hold her steady.

"I'm not done with you yet." I say as my hand clasps the base of her plug. Ever so gentle, I massage soft circles and coo, "Relax pretty baby." I press soft kisses to her stomach, her hips, before removing the toy. She looks at me, eyes half lidded, head slumped against the tiles.

"One more?"

She nods. So I give her a third.

———

AS WE TOWEL off Shae reminds me I promised we could go to the beach, and I relent. Layered in sweatshirts, we grab the bag of snacks and cross Ocean Drive. Shrubs and palm trees fill the patch of greenery before the sand. We walk the beach and I watch her amazement at each of the differently styled lifeguard towers.

When we hit the area near the playground, Shae darts off and I find her softly swaying on a swing.

Pulling a pre-rolled joint from my cigarette pack, I hold it up silently asking.

"Just weed?" she asks.

"Nothing else," I say, nodding in confirmation.

I pull my lighter out and flick the metallic gear. Holding the jay between my thumb and forefinger I inhale deeply and let the fire catch on the paper and flower. Smoke fills my lungs and then I lean forward, kissing Shae while exhaling the smoke directly to her.

I pass the joint her way, and sit on the swing next to hers. We continue to take hits and pass between us while drifting with the playground equipment.

Eyes on the sky, despite the way the neon lights of Ocean Drive obscure the stars, Shae gives a long, relaxed sigh. Her smile reaches from ear to ear, the corners of her eyes crinkling. Her head falls back on another exhale and she says, "I'm going to do it. Do you hear me universe? I swear to you, I am!"

"That is ominous, what are you plotting? Does it involve my body being dumped in the ocean with organs missing?"

She laughs, full throated. "Why are you still convinced I want your kidney?" She takes a long drag of the jay, and hands it back to me.

"No. I'm going to be as infamous as Emily; I'm going to open my own firm. I'm going to have people fresh out of college clamoring for the grunt work at my company the way I fought off twenty bitches for this job. I'm going to know how to elevate my clients, keep their secrets, and control the narrative better than anyone," she declares, not letting there be any waiver to her statement.

She swings back and forth a few times then pauses and turns. "What about you?"

"I'm going to have the hottest restaurant turned club since Tao. It'll be a fusion of the foods I grew up on and the foods I love. I'm going to be in AC, LA, Vegas. Oh, I'm going to take Vegas by storm someday," I say, grinning at the sky.

"I'll be your rep," Shae says with a far-off dreamy look in her eye.

"How can you be my rep if you said we can't talk after today ends?"

"Today?" she asks, eyes glazing over and I'm unsure if she's confused or stoned.

"Today is Christmas, Blondie," I say shining the time on my phone her way.

She reaches out and takes the phone and looks at it, eyes squinted into tiny slivers. "No way." She shakes her head and her hair flies around in the ocean breeze. "Time is a fake construct anyway."

When she passes back the phone, I take her hand and pull her swing closer to mine.

"Last hit?" I offer, turning the joint so the filter faces her and blow the smoke her way. We share the air, the tingling sensation between us increased by the quality flower.

Stomping out the final ember, I go to toss the last bit in the trashcan.

Approaching her swing, I wrap a hand around each chain to slow her motion and stare down at her. Those large, dreamy eyes. The long lashes framing them. Her pouty lips, full and soft.

"Pretty baby, how am I going to find you to be my rep when our careers get bigger if you won't let me get your full name, phone number, or anything?" I ask, voice laced with longing for there to be more time.

"You're a smart man, you'll figure it out. If it's meant to be, it'll happen. So it will," she says, smiles, and stands leaning in to wrap her arms around me.

We stand there, under the moon, holding each other in the stillness of the night.

"Come on, let's walk," she says, lacing her fingers with mine and I follow her to where the sand is packed from high tide. We walk north toward the next lifeguard stand, climbing onto the deck. In the dark of night, with nobody but the stars to hear, something shifts.

shae

SITTING on the deck of a colorful hut and talking about career dreams feels safe. There's nobody to one up me. I can breathe.

"My older sister is this bombshell Harvard psychologist," I admit sheepishly. "Then, it's me. With my state school bachelor's degree, sorority life, and reputation as the dumb party girl. Next is Tal, who is getting a masters in a fifth-year program. They are some sort of genius do-gooder and a major queer activist. Who isn't my sister now, but my sibling. I'm sure I'll fuck that one up a bunch more times. Not because I don't care about her—them. Because I keep fucking it up. They were my baby sister for twenty-one years, and now, they aren't. Then, there's the baby. He's the baby, but he's also graduating as Valedictorian, already accepted to a joint program to take him through his doctorate in veterinary medicine at fucking Cornell. I hate going home for things like Christmas when we don't even celebrate it."

Simon cuts off my ramble, giving a slight elbow to my side and says, "Movies and Chinese food is a way to celebrate. It's Jewish American history." His tone is gentle despite teasing.

"Fine. Despite it seeming super fucking arbitrary to come

home in December when we just did stuff in the fall," I correct myself.

"Can I take you out tomorrow for movies and Chinese food anyway?" Simon asks, pushing his lip out as far as he can.

"Well, obviously. I still want my noodles," I say with a low grumble from my stomach. Opening the backpack, Simon runs his hands through and pulls out a few bags.

"No noodles here, but how about… apricots? Pistachios? Dried mango?" he offers for me to choose first.

I take the bag of pistachios and open them. "Thanks."

We shell nuts and continue to compare our favorite dishes when ordering Americanized Chinese food. Simon shares some adorable story about how this all came to be, between the history of San Francisco's Chop Suey to the Manhattan origins of General Tso's Chicken.

"So, is that what you did with your family too?" I ask, mostly to be polite and also because this tiny gnawing on my insides. Like someone is poking me over and over, trying to whisper during a test and ask for answers. I might actually want to know more about this ink covered, storytelling, smoking, not-so-typically nice Jewish boy.

"Well, most of my family is back in Los Angeles. My parents are pretty religious, so they don't love all these things about my lifestyle. The tattoos…" he says, drifting off.

"The eating trief," I add teasingly.

"They know that I don't have a strictly Kosher business. I said it's because I can reach more people this way. They also really don't like—" Simon pauses and swallows thickly. "They don't love that I'm in my thirties and unmarried when so many of the people I grew up with are the parents of rising middle schoolers by now. It just wasn't my path. I'm just… I— I know I believe that there's something bigger than me. I don't think it cares about my body art or which foods I eat. I think it cares more about the kind of person I am." He worries his lip.

"I like that," I tell him simply. There's really not more to add, or any reason to disagree. "Our mom grew up Orthodox, but left. She's the one who pushed my sister to date her non-Jewish boyfriend. Said that our destiny doesn't always show up how we expect it to. Except, I think Nessa gets away with it because of how they see her. I don't know if she'd have been so lenient with me. I'd love to see her face if I brought you home."

Dropping a finger to my nose, in a slight boop motion, Simon teases me. "That, pretty baby, would involve telling me not only your last name but their names."

"Also, why are we discussing me again? This was supposed to be about you," I argue.

"Well, it's been about you a little bit," he says, then his mouth splits into a grin. Winking he softens whatever guard I was trying to reestablish. His long arm wraps around me on the side, and he continues to tell me about his siblings. Bekah, who works during the day in the business office at Sin, lives here in Miami. She and her husband and their children. There's too many names, ages, professions to remember but I ask questions and nod or laugh at the appropriate times to each story.

"Do you want that, then?" I ask. The sky is turning a shade of blue that suggests dawn will begin to creep in. We've spent the whole night talking about everything. Talking about nothing. Our backgrounds, our hopes, our dreams.

"Want what? Kids? Maybe, it wasn't as important as traveling. Eating. Meeting new people. But I've done so much of that. I still want the big cities, but maybe. Yeah. I wouldn't be against it. You?" he asks, eyes lingering on the horizon.

"I don't know. It might not be for me. I want to create something that wouldn't let me be very present as a mom. I've got time though. Maybe I'll change my mind," I say with a shrug. It's about as committed as I can get right now to the idea of a family.

"That's fair, what are you? Twenty-three?" Simon asks.

"A lady never tells," I say without a second thought.

"Ah, still the mystery woman. Alright Blondie. Well, I am thirty-three," he says mimicking my nonchalance.

"Look," I say thrusting a hand toward the ocean. The sky is brighter still and we can see a series of fins breaking the water in the distance. They begin to create a series of arcs bouncing in and out of the water gracefully.

"Oh! It's dolphins, oh wow," I exclaim.

Standing to get a better view, I lean over the lifeguard hut railing. Simon comes behind me, wrapping me in his muscular, inked arms and sighs. "Beautiful."

Except when I turn, he isn't watching the dolphins, he's watching my reaction. There, under the rising sun, I kiss this man knowing that this is absolutely a story I will never want to forget.

simon

AFTER WATCHING the dolphins at sunrise, we make our way to the hotel. I slip the concierge a bill with my handshake to have breakfast delivered right away, knowing the crash is coming. After overstuffed omelets and toast, that's exactly what happens.

Waking up in the early afternoon, I plan the remaining hours out as carefully as possible. There's the swanky Chinese food place that is like a step back in time sporting red interiors, potted palms, and paper lanterns. Gold tassels and embroidered dragons on the decadent silk fabrics throughout the building.

"Time to get dressed up, Blondie," I say before giving her a kiss, then two, three, all over her face until she's swatting me away playfully.

"Okay, alright, fine," she relents and I capture one more kiss on her soft pout.

Stepping back, her messy bun and the tangled sheets hold my attention like a moth to a flame. Her warmth, passion, and fearlessness cause every cell of my being to demand I try to show her what could be. It's illogical, but she feels like she's already mine.

"Wait here, I'll get ready," she says and struts naked to the bathroom, closing the door and I hear the lock click. I sit, scrolling my phone and answering all the neglected messages from the last day or so. When the bathroom door slides open, she's a vision in creamy white. The skirt comes up high on her stomach while the top is cropped short letting a thin line of skin peek through. Chic and simple with a neutral tall shoe with some kind of basket look. She's a stunner but it's the red that does me in. Her bag is red and so are her lips. Looking at her forces me to adjust myself when I stand.

"Damn, pretty baby," I exhale sharply. "I'd almost prefer to skip the reservation and put you on your knees. I'd love to see that lipstick wrapped around my dick. Think we'll have time before you call the timer off here?" I'm hoping to play it cool and hide my disappointment that this will end soon.

The entire drive to LiShang's my mind races along with the speedometer. I should tell her I'd like to see where this could go. I should take a hint and use this to start dating for real, at least not if I want to be someone different than Eli eventually.

I should ask her to take me on as a client to keep her close. Can she do that?

"Slow down, and that's coming from me," Shae cries. I watch as the numbers dip from over 120 MPH down toward 100 MPH, and with it so does her tension.

"Shit, sorry. Figured if these were our last few adventures, I'd show you what the car can do." I try to shake off acting so careless. Truthfully, I've never driven that fast. One hundred, sure. That high over? I'm a little shaken too.

I'm so lost in my head all of dinner that I'm fairly certain I've started to squander whatever is left of this little fling.

"So, movies?" she asks me, brow quirked. "I mean, if you're too tired, or want to go our separate ways now. I understand. No hard feelings. Truly. This has been amazing, Simon. Better than I could have hoped for."

Shit, I haven't told her what I want. I need more time.

"We still have to go to the movies, pretty baby. That's the deal. A full Jewish Christmas." I force a smile because we need to see this through. I need to see this through. We can't part yet. I need to get her to at least consider it.

Maybe we'll drift over time.

Maybe, just maybe, she's the woman I've been searching for all along.

GLANCING at the ticket for our assigned seats, I make sure to walk carefully with all I'm holding. My arms are full of popcorn, candy boxes, and a cola slush drink each—mine with the cherry mixed in.

"Here. Row D," she says pointing to the large letters on the floor.

"Sweet, scooch in Blondie."

Shuffling to the correct pair of seats, I swing the arm rest up to make snuggling and snack sharing easier. I wrap my arm around Shae, her head rests against my chest making every cell of my being scream at me. Stretch this day out as long as you can. Don't let her go, her touch makes you tingle like they talk about in movies.

I press my lips to her forehead, giving soft and sweet kisses hoping to somehow have these thoughts enter her mind from my touch.

Her hands slide over my thigh, and I watch my linen shorts produce a perfect outline of my rock-hard manhood. I stifle a groan into her hair. My words growl, "They haven't turned the lights down. Naughty girl, Blondie, Santa is never going to come if you do that."

"Wasn't trying to make Santa come. Just you," she purrs back while stroking me.

"In my pants?" I ask grabbing her wrist and lacing our fingers together hoping to at least delay her until the lights lower.

She gives a throaty laugh and someone in the theater shushes us loudly, the voice firm like an old school librarian. That makes our laughter increase, until we're panting and wiping away tears.

Shae loosens her hand from mine, then picks up the chocolate candies and mixes a handful with popcorn before tossing it in her mouth. I take a few sour gummies and offer the bag to her.

Thoughts scramble in my brain during the previews while I take her in fully. I try to memorize everything from the soft blonde hair pulled into a low bun to the way her tiny frame fits against my body. I study the curve of her button nose, the warm honey glow of her eyes and the long dark lashes surrounding them, and how since she got sun the faintest sprinkle of soft freckles have appeared. I watch her long, thin fingers and the soft pink round nails that start to trace my leg again. She is tracing the lines of the end of my thigh tattoo and over my shorts, her smirk growing as my cock thickens and presses against the fabric.

I kiss her ear, and let myself release the quietest whimper before pushing my lips to the pulse jumping from her neck. "Blondie," I exhale her name a mix of reverence and warning.

"You promised to finger fuck me all over this city, but so far it's been really proper hotel fucks and some flirting with trouble elsewhere. Where is your sense of adventure?" she says.

With that, I pull her halfway into my lap and run a hand from her neck down her chest. I cup her breast and squeeze, tightening my fingers to pinch where her pierced nipples press against the white fabric of her top.

I tickle and tease her stomach exposed from the crop top with gentle swirls along her soft skin. My fingers trace along her back, nestling closer between us. We shift slightly, allowing me to pull my arm across her front. Dipping my hand into the waistband of her skirt, I glide the pads of my fingers over her smooth skin. The tip of my middle finger finds where her body creases and I press over the textured ridges and reach the pool of her arousal, dragging my finger through and then up over her clit once more. She bites my ear, giving a heavy exhale and encourages me to keep going.

I'm rocking my fingers against her center, increasing the drip of her arousal against my hand at an even pace. With each movement forward and back, she kisses and sucks harder on my neck. With two fingers pushed in hard, curled toward where my palm grinds her clit, I feel her arousal coat my hand more. She opens her mouth to vocalize how the pleasure impacts her, but stops herself with a bite to my throat. I'm convinced when I look later it will have bruised.

The old librarian voice screams a second shush into the dark and we both try to sink lower in the seat. Try to lower the sounds that shouldn't be audible over the movie blaring from the speakers.

I was confident we were getting away with this until a bright light starts to sweep the room side to side. Quickly removing my hand from her body, Shae's low grumble of disapproval is cut short when the light stops on us.

"Alright, kids, there's been some complaints about your behavior. Time to go," an elderly usher in the maroon theater polo says. Shae scoops her bag up, and I grab my drink before we go to follow. Heads low, we slink behind the gray-haired employee down the stadium stairs and then back up the ramp to the exit.

Once outside in the main lobby, I drop the soda in a trash can and the gentleman says again, "Time to go kids. You really can't be doing things like that in public."

"I need to hit the head," I say pointing over my shoulder to the sign for the men's room.

"Fine. Miss, please step outside the premises to wait."

I've been with this practical stranger for almost two full days and there was no way to ninja myself into the lobby for a private

106

bathroom break. My stomach gives me a reminder that as much as I want time to stop, my body still has to do body things.

"Yeah, sure." Shae's eyes dart around. She points to one of the long sets of glass front double doors and says, "I'll be... over there." She turns and walks toward the dark parking lot.

By the time I've finished up and washed my hands though, she's gone. My phone dings.

JAVI: Merry Christmas, Si. How was the night with the blonde chick?

Simon: I've been with her nonstop, but we were caught fooling around at the multiplex and got asked to leave. Now I can't find her.

Simon: Did I get ghosted while taking a shit?

JAVI REACTED: haha to Simon's text

shae

"I FEEL bad that I left him like that, but I had to, Sarah," I whine to my colleague as we unpack the remaining items into the business office at Devotional.

"You could have said goodbye," she exclaims, her eyes hard.

"Shit," I shout, interrupting the conversation.

"What is it?" Sarah asks, her concern laced with the belief I'm distracting her. So what if it's both?

"When I got in, I noticed that the dresses sent over included the wrong size on the main piece. Nobody was answering, it got too late on the twenty-third for folks to be working. It's the thirtieth and we never got it swapped. We *have to* fix this. Do you have her stylist on your work sheet?"

Sarah swipes across her tablet between apps and documents frantically. Her eyes widen and meet mine. "We're so fucked."

It's then that I see a message come across my screen.

SAUL: Hey kid, was hoping to talk to your boyfriend. I had some ideas for his expansion he mentioned. Do you know the best way to get hold of him?

Immediately I dig out my phone and Saul picks up on the first ring. "Hey! There's my favorite new friend. How's it going?" He gives one of his deep, jolly laughs.

"Saul, not my boyfriend. Not even someone who I can get in touch with but I need something from you. Urgent. Do you happen to have any connects to designers?" I ask, my voice rushed.

"We'll circle back to the gentleman from Catskills Night, but actually. I know a guy," Saul says, the mirth in his voice never wavering.

simon

"I TOLD you I don't need you in the end," my Uncle Eli says glibly.

"And I told you, I'm here already. Tell the security guard that I can enter. *Please.*" I add please through gritted teeth. My blood is heated to a boil. I have to see her and beg for a chance to make this something real. I haven't been able to sleep, everything I've tried to cook is burning or falling flat. Since Shae left me inside the multiplex, I've been completely unable to function. I need to see her, even if it's a goodbye.

Through the phone, I hear my uncle barking orders around the kitchen. I can't take this anymore. "Eli, put me on the damn list," I roar into the phone.

The Devotional guard is looking at me funny, I'm about to be completely screwed. The car behind me beeps, and I see Shae's mentor-friend Saul. I press the button to disconnect the call on my steering wheel a little harder than necessary and wave out the window to him to back up. Once he's made space, I back my car out, park on the side and jog to him.

"Please, you need to help me. My uncle won't add me to the list, and I need to talk to her," I plead to the old man and a flamboyantly dressed companion.

"Why are you two not together?" he asks, skeptically. Protectively. I soften liking to see her protected.

"She disappeared in the middle of a date. We had only met the night before we had dinner with you," I admit on a long exhale.

"No way. There seemed to be something more there." Saul shakes his head at me.

"I know, she's something else. I need a chance to ask for us to try, or a goodbye, worst case. Please." I'm already bent low to the window of his car, it feels like I'm about to fall to my knees.

Pointing to the SUV behind us, the other man says, "Hop in with my assistants and we'll say you're with them."

"Thank you, oh. Thank you," I shout to the men and pop into an open seat next to an overstuffed rolling rack.

shae

WHEN SAUL AND *HIS GUY,* aka Guy Gunner, winner of a popular fashion design reality TV contest, come strolling in later that afternoon with their own rolling rack I watch the faces of my colleagues. The men stop in front of me and the team pushing the rack nearly comes up short and topples into one another. Sarah and I exchange an awkward giggle watching Gunner give an icy stare to the team before they disperse.

"So, this was the garment the store sent over for the end of the evening," I say handing the incorrectly sized piece to Gunner.

He exchanges a look with Saul before exclaiming, "She's lucky you have me on speed dial." Shaking his head, the long hair moves effortlessly around his oversized colorful glasses. Turning to me, Gunner says, "I'm going to be here when Emily arrives with the hosts. I'm going to say I begged to dress her because you called in a favor based on the disaster that was delivered. Do *not* tell her the size part, it will cause a meltdown of epic proportions. I have seen that woman skip meals over less."

"That can *only* happen if you explain why that handsome chef isn't still on your arm, though," Saul cuts in.

Crossing my arms in front of my chest, I say, "This feels like senseless blackmail Saul. I thought you wanted to have a mentee."

"Sure, and you know what happens after you age and have a name like mine? Everyone asks where Mrs. Claus is?"

Sarah and Gunner crumble into laughter. "Oh my god," Gunner shrieks.

"He does look like Santa, that's what it is," Sarah says to Gunner. These two now look thick as thieves.

"I told him we weren't exchanging information. I'm not really interested in a relationship until I show my family of brainiacs that I'm more than just a *party girl*. Also, why am I admitting this to such a random group of people?"

"Who else would you tell, Shae?" Sarah asks a little too pointedly for my liking.

"Nessa?" I say, but my voice wobbles knowing my sister and I are trying but I still get frustrated by her coming across as so perfect. "Well, Mateo."

Handing me my phone, she says, "Then you do that and we'll fix this dress situation."

Saul and I watch Gunner and Sarah leave. I dial Mateo on video; he picks up pretty quickly. "New little sis! What's shaking?"

"Umm, so I'm here with—" I pause trying to decide what to say.

"Hi, I'm Saul Nichlause, but you can call me Solly. I'm a retired PR pro your sister met on her flight who is currently trying to save her hide personally and professionally," he says cheerily.

"Okay," Mateo elongates the word, a bit concerned. "You good, kid?" Mateo asks, causing me to roll my eyes.

"I'm not a kid, come on. You know better than most," I say, arms crossed and the grouchiness coming through.

"Talk to me, what's up?" he repeats, still laid back and happy as ever.

"You tell him or I will," Saul says.

"You have me scared now, you into age gap romance?" he teases.

"Nessa have you reading her books?" I ask, partially in deflection.

"Audiobooks. Now out with it." He doesn't hesitate with the reply.

"Ugh, well. I met this guy, we were having a really good time over Christmas, and we agreed we were going our separate ways after. I kind of, um. I dipped when we got kicked out of the movies and I've been living life. But Saul is saving me with a wardrobe issue before Emily brings the hosts in for their fitting and he said he won't help if I don't talk to him or someone I trust about this stuff. So, I picked you."

Faintly, I hear my sister scream out, "Rude, Shae Shae, extremely..." She's cut off by what sounds like a hand over her mouth and a hush noise.

"Honored you know that game recognizes game, so tell me player, what about this man makes you want to actually give out your digits?" Mateo's goofy grin fills my screen.

Sighing, I share the parts of the expiration dating experiment that are appropriate.

"And the sex?" he asks, and despite not being close to prudish I feel my cheeks heat.

"She's the color of a lobster, so that tells us all we need to know," Saul answers for me.

"Take it from this reformed party hopping playboy, little sis. When someone will jump on board with your wild streak and support your dreams, you take it," Mateo says, ducking off camera and I hear a faint sound of him kissing Nessa and whispering to her.

"You're the one who supported my dreams," Nessa says to him.

"You are my dream, Ivy girl," Mateo replies.

"Well, thanks you two, this was just lovely. I'm going to let you get back to… whatever that lovey dovey stuff is. If we don't talk tonight, Happy New Year!" I cry and hang up the phone.

Turning to Saul, I grumble, "Happy?"

"Are you, kid? And don't give me the same as your brother-in-law. You're young enough to be my daughter. You're a *kid*. You trust me, right?" he says.

"Yeah, you have this Ancient Guide vibe in addition to the Santa thing," I say teasingly, loosening up.

"You don't have to give it all up for a relationship, not with the right person. I saw how that boy looked at you. You said you were strangers? I would have thought you knew each other forever," Saul says, not mincing words.

"Felt like it, honestly," I relent.

"Then maybe you should consider reaching out to the man, give him a chance to screw up before you end it," he says. Waving his hands in surrender he adds, "Just my two cents."

———

WHEN SHE ENTERS, Emily's face lights up. "Saul Saint Nichlause! Why do I have the pleasure of having a legend in my office?"

"Emily, you naughty mentee. You're in town and I find out from your team?" Saul calls to her.

My head moves on a swivel as I stammer, "You—and you—you both. You."

"Yes, Saul gave me my start in the industry many moons ago," Emily says approaching the man for a hug and a cheek kiss.

"You don't look a day older than when I hired you, my dear," Saul says with a wink.

"That would be the work of Dr. Morris, but thank you. I'll let him know you approve," Emily says.

"Is your mother doing okay?" Saul asks.

115

"You'd know better than me, weren't you in Philadelphia visiting her?" Emily deadpans.

Looking at Sarah intensely, I'm trying to communicate with my eyes but she's so overwhelmed by this revelation I'm worried her head is about to explode.

"Shae, Sarah, please take Gunner here to review the wardrobe and suggest his changes. Since we have an expert, let's be sure to get things made to fit our clients perfectly," Emily says dismissing us.

"Oh. My—" Sarah says, and Gunner finishes.

"—god, I know. I can't believe it either. Let's go, we have models to dress."

"Model, just one," I correct.

"Actually, you are needed in the kitchen, Blondie," Gunner says and I'm confused. My heart starts to beat faster. Is he here? It's already after ten PM on New Years Eve. His use of the nickname Blondie, plus the thought of Simon's uncle, and the conversation from earlier has me spinning.

Yet, when I get there, I don't see Simon. Just a slew of wait staff arguing over the order that they'll be rotating the different passed items. I clear up that hiccup and pop out to the dance floor. The lights are low, a series of bright colorful lights flash around the room and reflect off the shimmery silver dress I brought for the occasion.

I watch as the hostess comes out in her second to last outfit change and the way that Gunner elevated the simple silk mini dress through her accessories has me taking mental notes. The woman looks like a sexy version of Holly Golightly, there's multiple strands of pearls in sizes and lengths covering her back. They seem to be intentionally sitting like a choker, dripping down the material. When she swishes her body in time with her boyfriend's next song, I realize they aren't separate but a piece of the dress. He somehow created a unique look for her in the hour they were in the back.

Looking down at my tablet, I check off where we are in the series of events. The clock reads eleven-thirty-five. In a few minutes we need to move the crowd onto the patio and get them ready for the fireworks show. I'm about to tap into the specifics when Sarah appears and takes the tablet from my hands.

"You're needed by the entrance, sorry girl. I got this now," Sarah says.

Entrance? That feels like miles from here given the throbbing music and the bodies moving to it. "The entrance to this room?" I confirm.

"No, the main entrance," she says with a headshake.

Weird. I start to walk and hear the announcement over the speakers for guests to head to the courtyard. Working against the flow of traffic, I continue to bump into drunk and high party goers. Sweat is pouring out of me everywhere. It takes a solid ten minutes to cross the ballroom, and now I'm making my way along the long, dimly lit corridors following the orange glow of the exit signs.

The cool air conditioning hits hard, and mixed with the quiet stillness, an eerie feeling hits me. The closer to the front I get, I start to see a series of flameless candles illuminating the path.

There, at the front in a semi-circle of candles stands Simon. His gold rope chain is reflecting off the lights, his floral shirt is open one button lower than necessary, his strong arms crossed over his chest. He's staring down at his watch, anxiously.

"Two minutes until midnight," the host calls over the loudspeaker.

"Waiting for me?" I ask, our gazes locking in on each other.

His smile slowly builds, his softening expression inviting me in. I sink into the warmth of his presence, realizing how much I've missed it the last few days.

"I'm sorry I disappeared," I say softly.

"You only promised me Christmas, but I'd like to extend the deal. How do you feel about Valentine's Day? Or perhaps

Memorial Day? Maybe we can try this until *next* Christmas?"
Simon nervously rambles to me. I look up, and see one hand has
started to nervously comb his previously well styled hair.

"Perhaps," I say, and despite trying I can't suppress my smirk.

In the distance we hear the crowd counting down.

Ten.

He takes one step closer to me.

Nine.

I hold a hand out to his.

Eight.

He uses my hand to pull me in closer.

Seven.

He wraps another arm around me.

Six.

"I'm going to kiss you," Simon says, his mouth hovering over
mine.

Five. Four.

My heart races, what is he waiting for?

Three. Two.

Oh. His mouth claims mine. At first, it's soft, tempered. His
tongue parts my lips, searching. He finds my tongue, and we begin
to push and pull for control of the kiss. One of his hands finds my
ass, while the other finds its way to the back of my head,
deepening the kiss. My skin is tingling under his touch as his
hand moves up and down my backside.

"Happy New Year, pretty baby. What do you say?" Simon says
soft and sweet.

Recalling our first night together, I cock a brow and say,
"Depends. How good are your kidneys?"

With a laugh, Simon says, "Give me your phone Blondie."

I watch him dial a number, and pull his phone from his pocket.
Then I get my phone back and have a text.

. . .

305-122-5831: Hey pretty baby, it's Simon Hakimi. I'd love to come visit you in Philly and take you on a second date.

Blondie: Hi, I'm Shae Rabin. Miami has been fun. Philly, huh? I think I'd like that.

epilogue
shae

"TWO YEARS AGO, under the moonlight we shared a spliff and discussed our dreams," I whisper to Simon.

"I know you've realized I'm older than you but I didn't forget, Blondie. Can I take the blindfold off yet?" he says, his usual blend of irritation and admiration laced in his words.

"Let me finish," I say, nudging him with my hip.

His hands caress whatever he can get ahold of, which unfortunately for me isn't much, and he says, "Pretty baby, I *always* let you finish. Multiple times."

"Shh. Two years ago, you told me the dream was Vegas," I start again. Holding his hands and squeezing our fingers tight. "We talked about the ways we wanted to become the top of our fields, and tonight, we will have a grand opening for you. Here. In Las Vegas. I'm going to take off the blindfold in a moment, but I want you to not rush off to the kitchen to talk to the staff. I want you to take a deep breath to really absorb what you've created here with Play."

"You mean what we've created, this event wouldn't exist without my own full time powerhouse public relations manager." Simon smiles and squeezes my hands in return.

I lift the silk tie from his eyes, stashing it in my bag. "For later," I tell him with a wink.

He slowly turns in place, taking in everything from the leather and lace decor, the lighting, and the black and silver accents. As he faces the door his jaw falls.

"Look who made it for the party," Simon says before pointing at the double doors. Filing in are a series of familiar faces. Saul, in a bright red suit, walks in with Emily and Sarah. Behind them, I see our parents, his Uncle Eli. Simon's siblings, their spouses and the many nieces and nephews are tumbling in noisily. Nessa, Mateo, Tal, and Shua follow behind the kids.

Matty runs over, my nephew Ozzy in his arms. "Tita Shh Shh," the little boy shouts and leaps from his dad over to me.

"What's up rock star?" I ask catching him. He tries to mold his fingers into a horned rock sign, but it's a pudgy mess.

"Rock on Tita, this is magic," Matty says, giving me a one armed hug as he grins wide.

Nessa wraps her arms around us all and looks around. "This is crazy beautiful, who are we going to get to meet tonight?"

Simon slides up alongside me, and we exchange a conspiratorial look. "Aba," he calls and both our fathers look over at us.

"Aba, would you be disappointed if we had a little surprise for you *and* you saved a little bit on having four weddings to throw?" I ask, trying to make the most sweet and innocent face possible.

"Shae Eliana Rabin, what did you do?" my dad booms, and I look at where my left hand is in Simon's right. I realize in the low lighting, and with our tattooed rings it might not be so obvious.

The room has gone quiet and everyone looks waiting for my reply. "I um, well, I kind of," I stammer nervously. I clear my throat, and look at Simon for help.

Simon shouts to the room, "I'd like to introduce you all to the most important member of my team, Mrs. Shae Eliana *Hakimi*." He smiles wide, my heart races like the first time I saw him.

The bartenders must have heard the announcement, because "Dreaming" by Blondie begins to play. The opening lines about meeting in a restaurant, the movies, the dreaming. It's like the song foretold our festive little fling that turned into a lifetime of happiness.

The family swarms in and a disco ball lowers from the ceiling, illuminating us all with flecks of glittering light.

Nessa grabs my hand, searching for a ring and looks with a frown. "That's pretty permanent, you know?" she says examining the SH tattooed on my finger.

"So is marriage," I say, shrugging off the commentary. I'll never shake her overprotective ways, but I love her all the same.

"Very true. I'm surprised you didn't request something sparkly," Nessa teases.

"You mean like this?" Simon says, swooping in with a velvet box. Opening it, I find a large bright green emerald sitting on a band of diamonds.

He takes the ring and places it on my right hand, saying, "Until the ink has fully healed keep it here okay? I got you something else too. Something you've been asking about since we visited Rooster Alley." He winks and pulls out a second box that contains a long strand of pearls.

The two of us cannot contain our laughter, and I watch as Mateo giggles and steers his family away to give us a moment.

"A pearl necklace?" I finally say between giggles.

"The first of two tonight, if you're up for it, *Mrs. Hakimi*." He pulls me in for a kiss, deep and slow.

"You know I'm always up for anything when it's with you," I say.

The night continues with a full tour of the new location, dinner, drinks, and a little wedding cake. When we're all drunk, sleepy, and hearts are full, we say our goodnights promising to meet for the breakfast buffet tomorrow.

When we reach the elevators, Simon puts a key in and takes us to a different floor than yesterday.

"Where are we going? What happened to our stuff?" I ask.

"It's all there, don't worry baby," Simon says kissing my forehead.

The elevator opens and we're greeted by a series of doors to suites. "Mateo upgraded us when I told him why they couldn't miss this with the baby."

"Whoa" is all I can manage when we open the double doors. The living room has a balcony to the Strip and we can see all the lights. There's an ice bucket with chilled champagne waiting for us outside.

Popping the cork and filling the coupes, we toast to a long life full of wild antics. Then, I sink onto my knees. "Mmm, so, husband, how do you feel about a little exhibitionism?"

"If there's one thing we've really mastered, wife, it's figuring out how to get off almost anywhere," he replies.

I lower the zipper of his pants, his cock springing free, hard and proud. I grasp it with my right hand, watching the glimmer of my new ring as I work his length. "Almost," I repeat. I lick the crown of his erection briefly. "Still no luck with the movies though."

On that, he thrusts forward and I take him in by hollowing my cheeks and relaxing my throat. He pulls back and looks at me for the shortest moment. I meet his eyes through the thick mascara coated lashes.

"Dress down, baby, I promised you a second pearl necklace tonight," he grunts.

I quickly obey, and am seated in only my bra and heels before him.

"Fuck, you really never wear underwear, do you?" he groans.

I reply by pulling him by his ass back toward me and taking him fully down my throat once more. I continue to lave, tease,

123

and lavish him with each stroke of his length until he's spilling across my chest.

"Now you need to clean up your mess, I'm your wife not your maid," I say as I discard my bra and make my way to the shower with the oversized central rain feature and multiple personal sprayers. Bringing the water to warm, steam filling the room, it's a little foggier than I anticipated.

Simon approaches me pressing us together, chest to chest. Despite having just orgasmed, he is half-hard again. Pressing himself between my legs, I feel my wetness pooling. The more he rubs against my center, the wetter I become. The wetter I feel, the harder he grows, until he's pushed me up onto the countertop and notches himself at my entrance. It's hard, fast, and a little wild, just like us. Just like our love story.

Once we've washed, we lay naked in the king-size bed snuggled together.

"I love you, Simon, I'm so glad your uncle ruined a couch two years ago at The Devotional."

"I love you too, Shae like where the Mets play. I'm *more* glad you finally gave me your name," he replies, kissing my temple.

"I love you so much, I stole yours instead," I say before we kiss again. We spend our first Christmas as a married couple the same way we spent the one when we met, chasing our dreams and giving each other orgasms between.

So much for just a festive little fling, it looks like there's a lifetime of this to look forward to instead.

the end

before you go:

Thank you so much to every reader for giving me your time. If you enjoyed this book, please consider rating and reviewing it online.

My books would not exist without the support of a group of truly amazing people.

I'm going to use this note to gush about The Man behind Mr. Smutty Jess Mariano for a moment. It's been a wild few years since I first took a gummy, got an in-home Mother's Day massage and texted "I had the wildest idea, can I just type for a bit or do we have plans?" From that moment on, he's been my biggest supporter. This man saw a dating profile with a joke about buying things at bookstores and promised a stranger he'd build her a library. For nearly ten years now, over the span of four homes, he's met that promise in bigger and better ways. There is no way I could do this without you as my person. Thank you for being you.

To Sammie and Britini, thank you for being my critique team here. I love how much you've loved these two, and I'm so lucky to be on this weird, gut wrenching, exhausting journey alongside such amazing writers. Annie, thank you for talking me through it when *that* scene overwhelmed me.

Emilie, I'm so excited we were able to work closely on this one. Your Glitter Pen is magical.

also by jordana blake

Flying

Flying Bonus Scene

available on www.jordanablakebooks.com

Fighting

———

keep in touch

Jordana's Newsletter

Jordana's Facebook Reader Group:

Jordana Blake's Framily Readers Group

TikTok & Instagram *@jordanablakebooks*

about the author

Jordana is a textbook Millennial: she has a Master's Degree in Social Work she'll be paying off in the nursing home, a history of changing careers, and obsession with 90s nostalgia, and cannot talk before coffee.